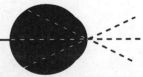

ALSO BY RICHARD PAUL EVANS

The Christmas Box

Timepiece

The Letter

For Children

The Christmas Candle

RICHARD PAUL EVANS

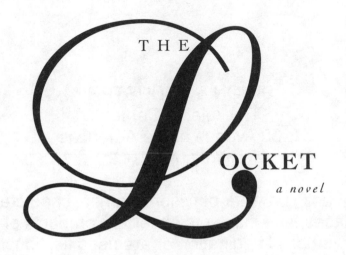

THE
LOCKET
a novel

DOUBLEDAY DIRECT LARGE PRINT EDITION

SIMON & SCHUSTER

This Large Print Edition, prepared especially
for Doubleday Direct, Inc., contains the complete unabridged text of the original Publisher's
Edition.

SIMON & SCHUSTER
Rockefeller Center
1230 Avenue of the Americas
New York, NY 10020

SIMON & SCHUSTER and colophon are registered
trademarks of Simon & Schuster Inc.

Manufactured in the United States of America

ISBN 0-7394-0085-1

ACKNOWLEDGMENTS

"It is not difficult to write a novel," wrote one novelist, "just slit your wrists and let them bleed over the pages." There is a lot of blood in this story. I am indebted to my grandfather, Marius O. Evans, and my friend, Tom Sanford, both of whom bled part of this story.

I would like to acknowledge the following: always, my friend and stellar agent, Laurie Liss, for her faith and love. My editor, Laurie Chittenden, for her valuable insight, inspiration, contributions, and love of my stories.

I am grateful for the chance to work with you, Laurie. Brandi Anderson for her excellent research assistance. My staff: Barry Evans, Melyssa Romney, Lisa May, and Elaine Peterson. David Rosenthal and Annik LaFarge for their continual support and commitment to success and excellence. Carolyn Reidy for her continual interest in my books. Thank you, Carolyn, for the cover. Isolde C. Sauer and Chuck Antony. Jackie Seow. To the Simon & Schuster sales team who makes it all possible. New York Times journalist Rick Bragg, a writer's writer, who in the course of one morning reopened a door I thought I had safely barred years before. Kris Rogers from Salt Lake City Legal Defenders. Detective Steve Cheever of the SLC Police Department. Ron Stromberg and Nancy Stallings of Adult Protective Services. Carin Hadley of Holladay Health Care. Kent Vandegraff of Weber State College. Christine Johnson of Heritage Management. My Colorado reading group(ies).

I note the passing of my dear friend, reader and Christmas Box House advocate, Ken Bell. You are loved and missed.

TO KERI

And to God for not taking her from me.

"Honour thy father and thy mother: that thy days may be long upon the land which the Lord God giveth thee."

–Exodus 20:12

"Believe.
Believe in your destiny and the star from
which it shines.
Believe you have been sent from God as an
arrow pulled from his own bow.

"It is the single universal trait which the great of
this earth have all shared, while the shadows
are fraught with ghosts who roam the winds
with mournful wails of regret on their lips.

"Believe as if your life depended upon it,
for indeed it does."

Excerpt from
ESTHER HUISH'S DIARY

CONTENTS

PROLOGUE

There are those who maintain that it is a shameful thing for a man to speak of sentiment, and the recounting of a love story must certainly qualify as such. But if there is virtue in stoicism, I do not see it, and if I haven't the strength to protest, neither have I the will to conform, so I simply share my story as it is. Perhaps time has thinned my walls of propriety as it has my hair.

If my narrative is, in fact, a love story, I suspect that the world will not likely recognize it—for pulp romances do not often push aluminum walkers or smell of peppermint oil.

Still, there are stories that refuse to be interred in silent graves like the lives who gave them breath. The story of Esther Huish is such—commenced and concluded in a town born of gold, a mining camp cradled in the lap of the Oquirrh Mountains in the remote, windswept ranges of western Utah: the town of Bethel.

Bethel is now a dead town, and its history is not one story but two, as towns may live more than once. In 1857 a tramp miner and sometime evangelist named Hunter Bell, expelled for card cheating from the nearby Goldstrike mining camp, was wandering in exile amongst the bulrushes of the Oquirrh foothills when he chanced upon a rich deposit of placer gold. Bell staked his claim and within a month was joined by more than sixteen hundred miners. Learned in the vernacular of the gospel, if not the spirit, Bell bequeathed the town the biblical name of Bethel—the House of God.

Though Goldstrike and Bethel were sister cities, they proved as different as siblings in character as in appearance. Bethel was staid and industrious. Her greatest structure was the local chapel, which, when resting off the sabbath, doubled as the town hall and a one-room schoolhouse. Conversely, Goldstrike's most resplendent structure was a honky-tonk piano saloon and brothel. It was a raucous haven of prostitution, gambling, and murder, aptly nicknamed by the Salt Lake City newspapers as Sodom West. As the larger and more accessible of the two cities, Goldstrike became the center of commerce on which Bethel relied for its train station, milling, and trade.

A year after the turn of the century, as gold production in both cities started to decline, tragedy struck Goldstrike. A fire, started in a saloon's kitchen, ravaged the mining town. It was followed by an ill-timed flash flood that collapsed most of the mines and all but washed away what remained of the once thriving township—a baptism of fire and water the area ministries claimed was apocalyptic, having prophesied that a great scourge was sure to befall the decadent town. Bethel, though spared heaven's wrath, was no longer accessible by railroad and died as well, leaving behind only those too old or too broken—like slag tossed aside after being purged of its wealth.

For nearly thirty years, Bethel (or Betheltown, as Esther and those indigenous to the small town called it) lay dormant, until 1930, when in the wake of the Great Depression, there was a resurgence of interest in the town's boarded-up shafts and Bethel was reborn as a Depression baby.

It was just prior to these days that Esther Huish arrived in Bethel—the young, beautiful daughter and sole companion of an elderly man seeking fortune as a miner. Prosperity eluded the man and time proved that his greatest wealth was his daughter, who, as he grew infirm, provided for him as the caretaker of the Bethel Boarding House and Inn. Esther was an elderly woman when I met her, in the last months of her life. She had become a recluse—preferring to our world an era that existed only in her memory and the diaries in which she chronicled those days. An era evidenced by a petite golden locket. It was an encounter that was to leave me forever changed.

I believe it a great irony that I learned of life from one dying, and of love from one so lonely.

To everything there is a season, said the Preacher, to every purpose under heaven— a time to get and a time to lose, a time to love and a time to hate, a time to dance and a time to mourn, a time to be born and a time to die. Those months with Esther were a season of all these things—and most important, the season I learned of faith, forgiveness, and second chances. One winter in a rest home called the Arcadia.

chapter one

Betheltown

"As I lie in bed listening to the toil of my body beneath the infirmities of age, my heart wanders again to Betheltown and I wonder how it is that, through the same sorcery of time that has brought me to my end, Betheltown has become less heartbreak than joy. And less memory than dream."

Excerpt from Esther Huish's Diary

Bethel, Utah. April 2, 1989

As the desert blurred past in the luminous hues of an impressionist's palette, Faye huddled tightly against the car door, her eyes closed and her coffee hair spilling over her face. The last of the music, frayed tones from a hayseed country station, had miles back degenerated into a storm of static, and now the only noises were the car's undulations over the primitive road and the occasional sigh of my sleeping companion. We had already traveled fifty miles past the last evidence of humanity, a rancher's lodgepole-pine fence, into the desert's blanched, stubbled plain, and Faye had not yet asked where it was that I was taking her. Her faith in our journey was not unlike her faith in our courtship, attributable only to some godlike quality of the female mystique—an unwavering virtue of hope and patience—that, if unable to predict our destination, found merit at least in the journey.

I had never been to this corner of the earth—only eight months previously, I hadn't even known of its existence—but the stories I had heard of the dead town had given it meaning, and I confess anxiety at its approach. I was told that the town, steeped in the foothills of the Oquirrh range, was constantly assailed by mountain winds. But there was no wind that day, and the spray of red dust in the car's wake hung in the placid air, liberated from a roadway not trespassed for a year's time.

I was glad for this day, for its blanched, cloudless skies, for though I embraced the land's immense solitude—felt akin to it—it would be foolhardy to venture so far from civilization with the possibility of becoming stranded on washed-out roads. Flash floods were common in these regions, and most of the ghost town's abandoned mines had decades earlier collapsed under their turbulent runoff. The wash of such cataclysm was a souvenir hunter's ecstasy of relics and coins and an occasional grain of gold. It had always been such with the town, as men came to take from the land or to take from those who had come to take from it, and even in death it was so.

Only, today, I had not come to take but to impart.

Before us the coarse road crested, then dipped into a barren creek bed surrounded by the pink clusters of spring beauties and the scattered stalks of bulrush that proved the creek still possessed occasional life. At the creek's shallow bank I left the car idling and walked to the rill and placed a hand to its stony bed. There was no trace of moisture. I examined our intended route, rolled back a single stone of possible hazard, then returned to the car and traversed the bed. A half mile forward, the timber skeleton of a gold mine's stamp mill rose from a mesquite-covered knoll—a wood-tarred contrivance of rusted wheels and cogs and corroded steel tracks over which ore cars had once rolled and men and horses had sweat. I glanced down to a crudely drawn map, astonished that after all these years,

and with a dying memory, Esther had remembered such landmarks so distinctly. I
wondered if she had just never left.

At the mill's passing I turned west and
coaxed my Datsun up the hill, where the
road vanished into a buckwheat-dotted plain
that spread infinitely to the north and south
and climbed the foothills of the mountain
into the town itself. As we neared the decrepit structures of the once-flourishing
township, Faye's eyes opened and she slid
up in her seat.

"Where are we?"

"Esther's hometown."

Faye gazed on in apparent fascination.
". . . what's left of it."

We passed the ornamental iron fence of a
cemetery. "Welcome to Bethel—the House
of God."

"This is where Esther was born?"

"She came here as a young woman." I
looked out at the desolate terrain. "Makes
you wonder why anyone would come here."

Faye turned to me. "Why are we here?"

"To fulfill a promise."

Faye leaned back in her seat, momentar-
ily content with my ambiguity.

I parked the car under the gnarled limbs

of a black locust tree near the center of the deceased town and shut off the engine.

The morning's drive had taken nearly two hours, but it was the conclusion of a much greater journey, one that had taken nearly half a year. A journey that began the day my mother died.

chapter two

The Arcadia

"The Arcadia is unlike that chill, tile institution that I was brought here from. The small difference between it and a sepulcher was movie night."

Excerpt from Esther Huish's Diary

Six months previously.
October 30, 1988. Ogden, Utah

For the third consecutive day, snow fell heavy in driven blasts that cloaked all that hadn't the sense or ability to come in out of it. From my perch at a shallow bay window, I watched the mortician's high-stepped approach through the piled snow. Tucked under the man's arm was a folded vinyl body bag. Midstep, the heavy man lost his footing, flailed, then disappeared in a sprawl of slush and powder, then rose again, cursing as he brushed down his charcoal overcoat. Moments later a gloved fist pounded against the door. The man was ruddy cheeked and broad faced. He was still breathing heavily from his hike, his breath clouding before him as I opened the door.

"I can't find the street numbers. This the Keddington place?"

"You have the right house," I said.

"Body inside, I reckon."

I glared at him. "My mother is inside."

The man kicked his boots against the threshold, then stepped past me into my home. He glanced about. The spartan room was carpeted in a well-worn shag of olive hue, and bare except for three humble pieces of furniture—a wooden armchair, a garish red-and-gold upholstered sofa, threadbare in its extremities, and a single brass-stemmed floor lamp, its shade burned through where it had once fallen against its bulb. The room was illuminated only from the window.

"Where's your mama?"

I pointed toward the darkened hallway. "The bedroom is there on the right."

The man unbuttoned his coat but did not remove it, and stepped in the direction of my gesture. I followed him to the doorway. Inside the dim room he moved toward my mother's body, shrouded beneath a hand-tied quilt of her own making. He pulled down the blanket, removed one glove, and placed two fingers beneath her chin, then looked down to examine her fingernails.

"When she go?"

I looked again at my mother's face. "Just a few minutes before I called," I replied, glancing up at the shadowed face of the mantel clock. "Maybe three hours . . ."

"Coroner been by?"

"The certificate's on the nightstand."

"Anyone else witness her passing?"

"No. We only had each other."

"I'm sorry," he said, and there was a trace of empathy in his voice. "No other family?"

"I have an uncle. But he's not family."

"Where's your old man?"

"He died a few years back." Then I added without thought, "Not that he was family either."

The mortician's brow furrowed. "How's that?"

I feigned the tipping of a bottle, a habit acquired through years of explaining my father's absence. "We hadn't seen him for more than seven years before he drank away his liver."

The man nodded empathetically as he removed his second glove. He stood and walked to the foot of the bed, drawing the quilt down with him. He lifted his bag from the floor and began working it up over her body.

"Don't mean to be judgmental, but for just losing your only family, you ain't seem much broken up."

I was too numb to feel slighted by his remark. "My mother has been dying since summer. There just aren't any tears left."

He closed the bag up over her head. "Yeah. Eventually it just give out." He stood back as if to examine his work. "There's a few papers you'll need to sign. Legal papers."

We walked out to the kitchen and he spread the forms about the drop-leaf table, pointing me to the lines that required signatures.

"This your place, or you rentin'?"

"It's mostly the bank's. But we put a down on it a few years back."

"Well, if you're thinkin' of sellin', I know a good realtor. They've been tearing down these places and putting up mini marts." He sniffed. "Reckon you'll be headed off anyhow."

"Why is that?"

"Just always happens that way. Demons will chase you off."

". . . Only the ones at the mortgage company. I haven't been able to work since she took to bed last summer. Between the medical bills and house payments, I'm pretty much buried." I signed the last paper.

"You got some employment in mind?"

"Whatever I can find. Work's a little scarce around here."

He reached into his coat pocket and took out a dog-eared business card, penning a phone number and address on its reverse side. He offered me the card.

"Are you hiring?"

"Nah. That's the number to a nursing home. The manager up there told me just yesterday that she needed help. Tell them that Roger sent ya up. They like me up there."

"I don't have any experience with that sort of thing."

"You been at your mama's side since last summer, you got plenty experience. Tell them I sent ya," he repeated. "I'm kind of a regular."

"What is the place called?"

"The Arcadia Care something."

I stowed the card in my shirt pocket and the mortician stood.

"Hate to impose, but could you lend me a hand here taking your mama out to the car? This blizzard has us shorthanded at the morgue."

We carried my mother's body out under pallid skies to the back of the station wagon. The mortician secured the tailgate, then took a brush from his front seat and scraped his windshield. I watched from inside the house as the station wagon fishtailed from the curb into the icy roadway and took my mother away. I closed my eyes and wept.

It was appropriate that Faye laid flowers on my mother's coffin before it was lowered into the frozen earth, as she had brought my mother flowers at each visit during the last months of her life. Perhaps even more appropriate, they were bluebells, for in the parlance of flowers, the bluebell denotes constancy and forbearance. The bluebell is metaphoric, too, of my mother's life, for once plucked, its nodding bells soon droop and the flower withers. I have seen photographs of my mother when she was a young and graceful woman with a beautiful face—an image she saw chiseled away a day at a time by the cold, sharp implements of travail. Her only sin, if it be deemed such, was in marrying a man who loved alcohol more than God and self, and the demons that haunted my father also tormented those he should have loved and sheltered. My mother sacrificed all to protect me from that torment, to fill her child's heart with hope when her own was broken. If I have accomplished anything in this life it is to her credit, not mine, and if there is love in my heart it is because she put it there. I do not know what requisite checklist is kept at heaven's gate or, in truth, if even there is such a realm, but if there is, I suspect it will be filled with people like her.

The instant of my mother's death should have been something indelible, something soulful like the opened-mouth wailing of the aborigines. Something worthy of a woman who suffered life's storms as a shelter for her only child and worried less about her hurt than that I might see her bleed. Her death should have been worthy of such battered nobility. Instead, I watched death's process with stoicism, and the final event seemed no more spectacular than the un-

easy breaths of the minutes or months pre-
ceding.

My mother had not died quickly, and my
agony of her loss, like her breath, had been
pilfered away a day at a time until all that
was left was silence and the intense loneliness of resolution. Maybe it was because I
had seen her die a thousand times already.
Maybe it was just that I thought anyplace
else had to be better.

During the last months of my mother's life, I
kept to her side, isolated from the outer
world and its movement, like the ice climber
who, in the shadow of the glacier's crawl,
seeks only to secure his own precarious
purchase. The one exception to my seclusion was Faye.

Faye had entered my world the previous
summer by way of Heller's Grocermart,
where I worked as a stock boy in produce.
She had come to the store with her sorority
friends, preppy, loud, flippant, and gorgeous. I stole glances at her as I stacked
grapefruit on an inclined produce shelf. She
suddenly turned toward me and we shared
brief eye contact before I turned away, embarrassed at being caught in my voyeurism

as well as my canvas grocer's apron. The next day she returned alone looking for okra, and in an act of rare gregariousness I mustered the nerve to ask her out—though it is possible that she asked me out. She later confessed that she had no idea what to do with okra, but had seen it advertised on a placard outside the store and found it as suitable an entrée as any.

We began seeing each other regularly about six weeks before my mother's illness took me from my job and the mainstream of society. I had gone to lengths to hide our poverty from Faye, and when I had not called her for a week, she hunted down my home in our ramshackle neighborhood. I don't know who was more mortified. I followed her eyes as she gazed upon our ragged home while I offered a belabored excuse for not calling. Faye was clearly affected by what she saw—horrified—and I was sure I had lost her. I lied that I'd call when things were better, knowing that she would act concerned because she was a good girl, but my call would never come and she would quickly paint over me. Though my heart ached, I would be lying if I did not admit that there was relief to get the inevitable over with. Rich and poor do not mix. And my family had always been poor. My father drank what little he earned and my mother worked where she could, hauling her child with her to homes where she would shine floors and windows for people that lived in neighborhoods like Faye's—where poverty was obscured through thick country-club windows and the needy were more of newsprint than of flesh.

When someone we love is dying, we do not ask doctors for a price list, and my mother's medical bills had forced me into still greater debt. I would have declared bankruptcy, perhaps should have, had my mother's ghost allowed. Even on her knees, my mother was a proud woman who "lived in no one's debt but the Lord Jesus'."

In truth, my financial circumstances were the more easily solved of Faye's and my differences, for all it takes to solve poverty is money. There were greater deficits left by my father's abandonment.

Some men become violent with drink, while others—the criers—turn their rage inward. Such was my father. Though he had never raised a fist, his abandonment was sufficient to take things from me that I could not explain or replace. But if he had left me broken, Faye made me feel whole. And this realization frightened me more than all my father's drunken binges, for I knew Faye could not last. I knew it from the moment we first kissed. I reminded myself as she comforted me at my mother's funeral. This was landscape I was certain of. I could see it. Her father demanded it. Faye was only a matter of time. So why, then, didn't she go?

The Arcadia Care Facility sat on a sloped parcel a mile up Ogden Canyon, housed in one of the city's oldest standing mansions—a gabled stonework edifice rising to bright red shingles three stories above the canyon roadway.

It was less than two weeks after my mother's death that I went to the nursing home seeking employment, leaving my car where the parking lot's snow had been plowed up into a six-foot bank. Despite the chill, occupying an inert rocking chair on the home's front porch sat the blackest man I had ever seen. He was scant of height and lean, and his face was tainted with silver stubble. His eyes were cavernous with age, which rendered them as black as a well of india ink. He wore a faded vermilion jacket and threadbare denim trousers—his right pants leg tied up above the knee where a leg had once been. A single crutch lay against the side of the chair and would have fallen had there been any motion. A thin stream of smoke curled from the tip of the cigarette that burned from his mouth. He looked impossibly old, I thought.

I tipped my head to the man. "Morning."

He remained silent; his ebony eyes flitted about but did not settle, quickly returning to the static white panorama that stretched before him. He suddenly broke out in a fierce cough. I walked past him into the home.

There is a distinct odor to most nursing homes—an olfactory soup of medicinal properties—but it was not so severe in the Arcadia, as if the walls of the old home breathed in the pungency and exhaled their own wooden bouquet. The foyer was broad, and at the east end was a curved, spindled staircase next to a modern elevator, where several residents in wheelchairs sat. To the rear of the foyer was a Formica counter, behind which sat a young, pretty woman dressed in hospital blues. She had thick, dark eyebrows and sienna eyes and cropped sable hair. Her complexion was sallow, more so in contrast to the darkness of her features. I guessed she was a couple years older than myself. She followed my approach with apparent interest.

"What can I do for you?" she asked sweetly.

"I've come to apply for a job." I fumbled inside my shirt pocket and extracted the mortician's card and set it on the counter. "Roger from the state morgue said I should come by."

She gave the card a cursory glance. "To help increase business, no doubt," she said sardonically. "You'll need to see our director. I'll see if she's available." She disappeared behind the counter through a back office door, returning a moment later followed by a corpulent woman with a pleasant face and a radiant mane of red hair with curls as wide as juice cans. The woman wore a luminous fuchsia blouse, partially concealed beneath her white smock; the ensemble was accented by thick plastic beads. "I'm Helen Staples. May I help you?" she asked, extending her hand.

"You are the director?"

"I'm the boss," she replied brightly.

"Roger Clemmens at the morgue told me that you were looking for help."

She lifted the card from the countertop, then looked me over. "Roger, huh? Have you any direct patient-care experience?"

"I've spent the last two years caring for my mother."

"Your mother is elderly?"

"She had terminal cancer. She died recently."

Empathy crossed her face. "I'm sorry to hear that." She handed back the card. "Come on back to my office."

I followed her to an adjacent room overcrowded with books and file folders and glossed paper boxes of medical supplies. There was a method to its disorder, and if things were in piles, they were, at least, in organized ones. Behind her wooden desk a metal radiator, painted the ivory of the walls, groaned beneath its task. Thumbtacked to the plaster wall was a large laminated calendar with illegibly scrawled notes indicating the month's activities. On the desk was an open box of powdered doughnuts.

Helen sat down across from me. "Tell me about yourself. Are you from the area?"

"I live down Twenty-fourth, just west of the viaduct, behind the Union Station." I was accustomed to receiving an adverse reaction whenever I shared my address, verbally or otherwise, but Helen showed no sign of trepidation.

"Are you a college graduate?"

"I was in college, but I had to drop out to take care of my mother. I'm hoping to start back next fall and work evenings."

"So you would like to work days until fall, then move to the night shift?"

"Yes, ma'am."

She seemed satisfied with the proposal. She leaned forward, laying her arms across her desk.

"What exactly did you do for your mother?"

"I was all the hospice she had, so I did pretty much everything. Cooked, fed, bathed, toileted her, helped her with her medications."

"Do you have any full-time work references?"

"I worked at Heller's grocery store for about a year. But they won't give much of a reference. I had to leave my shift several times because of my mother. My manager gave me a bad time about it. If I hadn't quit, I suspect he would have fired me."

She looked at me circumspectly. "I appreciate your candor, Mr. . . ."

"Keddington. Michael Keddington."

"Michael. You haven't hurt your chances with your confession. No one here is paid enough. You have to care about these people. Frankly, I could train a monkey to change bedpans, but if you don't care . . . well, I can't teach that." She suddenly glanced back toward the front counter, and I wondered if this was in reference to the young woman who greeted me.

"How much does the job pay?"

"Fourteen hundred a month to start, with a performance raise in six months. Plus meals in the cafeteria. Some don't consider that much of a perk."

"That's more than I made at the grocery."

"If that's satisfactory, when can you start?"

"Are you hiring me?"

"No offense to you, but we're desperate. We've been shorthanded for two months, so the sooner the better. We'll need to see that you're certified as a nurse's aide, but we can do that in-house."

"I can start right now."

She stood, evidently pleased. "Splendid. One of our aides called in sick, so I was about to change bedding. I'll have you accompany me. It will give you a chance to see the place and meet some of our residents." She stepped from behind her desk, looking me over for height. "How tall are you?"

"I'm about six foot."

"I'll get you a pair of blues, but until then you can just wear a smock." She removed the garment from a wood locker and handed it to me still on its hanger. I pulled it over my street clothes as I followed her out into the hallway. We paused again at the front counter.

"Alice, this is Michael. He'll be joining us as a CNA."

Alice smiled as if this was to her liking. She stretched forth her hand. "Welcome to our Greek paradise."

Helen did not smile, and I sensed tension between the two women. "Is Wilma's medicine in?" she asked.

"Not yet."

"Let me know when it's delivered."

"The very minute," Alice said buoyantly. She again smiled at me. "I look forward to working with you, Michael."

Helen started off, orating like a tour guide sans bullhorn. "The Arcadia is a county-operated extended-care facility. We have thirtynine residents here today; we can accommodate up to forty-six. Our population changes weekly. Most of our residents require around-the-clock supervision, though there are some here just because there is no place else for them to go. We keep six employees on staff twenty-four hours a day, not including the meal crew. The office, cafeteria, therapy, and recreation room are all on the first floor. Residents live on the second and third. It's not the best layout for a care facility, but the residents like it . . ." She pushed the elevator button and the door opened. ". . . it feels more like a home than an institution."

We exited on the second floor and Helen stopped to hold the door for a small, bent woman pushing an aluminum walker.

"How are you today, Grace?" she asked cheerfully.

The woman looked bewilderedly into Helen's face. "Who the hell are you?"

Helen smiled. "I'm Helen. I'm the director here."

"Oh," she said, and pushed on into the elevator.

"It's a daily event," Helen explained. We walked to the nearest numbered doorway. "This room is Stanley's." A wry smile crossed Helen's face. "You'll enjoy this." She knocked gently before slowly opening the door.

"Hello, Stanley."

Across the room an elderly man with tousled gray hair backed himself against the wall. Though stooped with age, he was still nearly a head taller than I. To his side was a nightstand crowded with religious icons and a plethora of candles of varying sizes and tints, none of which had ever been touched by flame. He stared at us with wild eyes, agitated at our intrusion. He suddenly erupted: "Depart, you filthy demons of the infernal pit."

Helen appeared unfazed by the attempted exorcism. "Stanley, we're going to change your bedding."

He snatched from the ledge a wooden cross and a large-print Bible, holding them both out at us. "I rebuke you, foul, dumb spirits." He pointed the cross at me, his eyes dully glowing. "Blasphemer!" he shouted. "I

have rebuked you, blasphemer! Depart! Depart!"

When I did not, he lowered his head and
side-shuffled to the corner of the room. He
sat down in a wooden chair and rocked forward and back, his arms crossed over his
holy paraphernalia. Helen waved me forward and we pulled down the sheets as the
man watched in agony as we performed the
demonic ritual. We finished the bed, emerg-
ing from the room with an armful of wadded
sheets. Helen was more amused with my reaction than Stanley's display.

"What do you think of Stanley?"

"Is that normal?"

"For Stanley it is. Actually, he was in rare
form this morning. He usually just damns me
to eternal hell." She added, "I think it would
have been a kick to see him twenty years
ago."

"He was a preacher?"

"An accountant."

As we walked to the next room a wheel-
chaired woman with oxygen tubing running
up to her nose followed me with her gaze.
She forced an awkward wink.

I smiled at the woman and she winked
again.

"What do I do if they're still in bed?"

"We usually have them get up. We reposition bed-bound patients every two hours to avoid bedsores. I'll have Alice show you how. She is one of our attendant RNs."

"Have you been here awhile?"

"Since the Arcadia opened. But I've worked in nursing homes since I was seventeen."

It took us almost an hour to work our way to the next floor. We started at the furthermost doorway on the hall.

"This next room belongs to Esther. You can expect her to be inside. She doesn't mingle much with the others."

"Why is that?"

"In part because she's now nearly blind. But she stayed apart before that."

Helen knocked on the door, then slowly opened it. Across the room, an elderly woman sat in a glider of stained maple, fervently crocheting. The room was smaller than the others, allowing only one bed. It had a vaulted ceiling and a gabled window well. The seated woman was not unattractive. Her hair was thin, turned the silver of platinum, and her skin was translucent, like fine porcelain, grown less opaque with years as it does with the elderly. Across her lap lay a rust-and-brown macramé afghan. On the wall above her head was a framed cross-stitch that read, *Old Age Ain't for Sissies.*The room was small and tidy, and a scented candle burned and filled the room with lilac. A steel-framed hospital bed sat in the center, offset by a walnut bureau with an ornately framed looking glass. The cabinet's antique veneer was covered with a white lace embroidery beneath pastel-labeled bottles of perfume and ointments, an aged, leather-skinned Bible, and three picture frames of varying sizes. The center picture was in a horizontal frame of varnished hardwood, an aged photo of five sullen-faced soldiers clad in the vestments of some war. The photograph to its left was of more recent vintage—a soldier wearing a newly issued uniform and the imperious smile of youthful zeal, both untainted by the actuality of combat. The third picture, set in a rococo pewter frame, was of a beautiful young woman.

"Hello, Esther," Helen said.

"Is there somebody with you?" the elderly woman asked.

"Esther, this is Michael. Michael will be giving us a hand here from now on."

"He is a new employee?"

"Yes. He just started today."

Her hands continued in fluid reverie. "I suppose that will be all right."

Helen walked to the candle and blew it out, confiscating the book of matches that lay next to it. "Esther, you know you're not allowed to have an open flame without someone being in the room with you."

"It was starting to smell like an old folks' home in here."

Helen faintly grinned, then said to me, "Go ahead and finish the third floor, then find me downstairs when you're done."

In Helen's absence the room fell silent, and the woman returned to her own seclusion as if all humanity had left the room with Helen. I began to dissect the bed while the woman's nimble hands continued, methodically creating something she could not see. I drew down the sheets, then gathered them into a pile. The silence grew uncomfortable.

"I'm Michael," I said.

"So I heard."

I glanced at the portraits on her bureau. "Are these pictures of your family?"

There was a protracted pause. "Is that of concern to you?"

I turned back to the woman. "No. I was just making conversation."

She did not speak again, so I aborted the attempt and went back to my work, laying the new sheets on the naked mattress.

". . . One of them is—the photograph of the soldiers. That is my father to the left."

I looked back at the photograph, studying the somber-faced trooper. "They never smiled back then."

"They smiled all the time. Just not for photographs."

I looked back at her, not sure if I should risk another question. "This other picture here, is it of your husband?"

She did not answer immediately, then demurely replied, "No. It's not."

I turned my attention to the last of the pictures, a posed, ancient portrait of a woman. Her face was delicately shaped, pale and smooth as if sculpted of marble.

"That last picture is of me," she said without prompting. "I was beautiful at one time."

I turned to see if I could distinguish the resemblance.

"Have you any photographs?" she asked.

I thought the question odd for a blind woman. "Not with me."

She looked disappointed, as if she had been cheated. "What do you look like?"

"I'm six foot. I have brown hair and blue eyes."

"How old are you?"

"I'm almost twenty-two."

"Are you married?"

"No."

"Are you homely?"

At that I wished I had not drawn her from her solitude, which perhaps was her intent. "No."

"You sound reasonably attractive," she said curtly.

"How does one sound attractive?"

"Close your eyes when the television is on. You can tell. Except that everyone on the television is usually beautiful. That's why they're there. You can bet no one in here would wind up on the television. Except maybe you. You sound attractive."

I finished tucking in the corners of the bed. "Alice is attractive."

"They would never put Alice on television with that scowl."

"How do you know she scowls?"

"She speaks with a scowl."

"I've never seen her scowl," I said.

"You will."

I gathered up the sheets. "I better go now."

"You better."

"I'll see you later."

"I suppose that can't be helped."

I gladly left the room and made my way through the rest of the floor without incident, with the exception of one female resident's screaming "Fire!" when I entered her room. She continued for about a half hour in increasingly shrill bursts until Alice came to my rescue. When I had finished the floor I carried an immense bundle of linen to the laundry room, then found Helen downstairs in the dayroom, where a half dozen residents had parked their wheelchairs around a color television to watch *Hee Haw.*The set's volume was peaked, so that the twang of banjos echoed throughout the room.

"All done?" she asked over the din.

"I got every bed I could find."

"How was your visit with Esther?"

"Tolerable."

"That bad?"

"She's a surly woman," I observed.

Helen accepted my assessment with lightness. "Those with the softest hearts build the hardest shells." She smiled. "You'll have to get used to her. She needs to get out of her room more, and I need you to walk her."

Walking her was a charge I did not look forward to. The rest of the afternoon I followed Helen around as she introduced me to duties and patients with equal passion. As garish as she appeared, Helen was genuine and kind and treated the residents with dignity and their antics with humor. At five o'clock Helen gave me my weekly work schedule and clocked me out for the day.

I arrived home to find Faye's silver BMW sided up to my front curb, exhaust coming from her tailpipe. Faye was inside the car, fully reclined. She wore a long coat and was reading a book. I knocked on the window and it startled her. She smiled as I opened her door.

"Hello, handsome," she said, kissing me. "Where have you been all day?"

I crouched down on my heels against the curb. "I started my new job."

"At the nursing home?"

"They were pretty desperate."

Faye smiled contently. "I'm happy you got it. A nursing home is a better fit than the produce section of Heller's." She stretched her arms around my neck. "You're very compassionate, and eggplant doesn't appreciate it."

I noticed the pile of books on the passenger's seat. "How long have you been waiting?"

She reached forward and turned off her ignition. "About two chapters of Kant."

I took her hand and helped her from the car. "Why didn't you wait inside?"

"I did. But it got too cold inside, so I came out to warm up."

We started toward the house.

"I found out last night that my father has been listening in on our calls."

I looked at her incredulously. "He has?"

"Based on my conversation with him last night, it appears so."

"You'd think a chief surgeon would have something better to do."

"Than look after his little girl? Not likely." She glanced down at the waxed bag of doughnuts I had picked up on the way home. I tilted it toward her.

"Doughnut?"

"Tell me that's not dinner."

"You don't like doughnuts?"

"I'm making dinner tonight."

"You need ingredients to make dinner."

She opened the unlocked door for me. "I know. I went shopping."

Weeks before, I had given Faye a key to my house, and this was not the first time that she had stocked the shelves. I took Faye's coat, then went and turned up the thermostat. Faye went to the kitchen.

"Heller's had a special on salmon. I thought I'd make spinach fettuccine and salmon. I hope that doesn't upset your system. It's hard cooking for someone whose diet consists solely of bagels and sugared cereal."

". . . and doughnuts."

"And doughnuts. Nutritionists should do a study on you."

I set the table and poured white grape juice into the glasses. Faye finished simmering an Alfredo sauce and we sat down to eat.

"I'll be so relieved when this quarter is finished. I don't think I've ever worked so hard."

"At least there's Thanksgiving break to look forward to."

"And I am. Are you still agreeable to having Thanksgiving dinner with my family?"

"I think this is your father's idea. He hasn't had enough chances to humiliate me recently and he's afraid he'll get rusty."

"Not a chance. He practices when you're not around." Faye smiled sympathetically. "He just needs to get to know you." Faye's optimism bordered on the ludicrous. "Any word on your scholarship?"

"Nothing since the first cut. I have an interview before the university scholarship committee the first week in December."

"I have a good feeling about it," she said.

"If it doesn't happen, I could always qualify for financial aid."

Faye frowned. What I considered pragmatic, she labeled as pessimism.

"Tell me about your first day at work."

I set down my fork. "It was entertaining. One old guy tried to cast us out of his room like evil spirits."

"Did it work?"

"Eventually. But not before I changed his bedding."

"Is that what you do? Change bedding?"

"And other glamorous chores, like changing bedpans and shaving ninety-year-old legs."

"I think it's wonderful that you're helping people." She paused to sip her juice. "What are your coworkers like?"

"I've only met a few of them. But they were really helpful." I speared some salmon. "Outside of the residents, I think I'm the only male there."

She looked up jealously. "Maybe it's not such a good job for you."

After supper we left the dishes and retired to the couch and television. Faye fell asleep in my arms. I woke her as Johnny Carson was signing off.

"Do you want me to drive you home?"

"No." She sleepily kissed me, then leaned back into me. "I shouldn't have stayed up so late. It's Shandra's wedding tomorrow."

I wrapped her in her coat. "If it's any consolation, you went to bed an hour ago," I said. I opened the door and the nighttime winter air braced us as we walked out to her car. Faye shivered as I unlocked her door. Her breath froze before her. "You'll meet me at the reception tomorrow night?"

"I'll get there as soon as I can."

"I'll be waiting for you. It will be a really nice affair." She looked at me and again shivered. "I can't believe you came out here without a coat."

I wrapped my arms around myself. "I'm thick skinned," I said. We kissed again, then she slid down into her car and I shut her door behind her. The phone rang a few minutes after she left. Faye's parents always worried when Faye was in my neighborhood after dark.

chapter three

Henri

". . . Not all heroes are painted on white stallions."

Excerpt from Esther Huish's Diary

The stone-faced mansion that housed the Arcadia was built in 1818, when Utah was still a territory—unaccepted by a Union that in a generation would seek divorce from itself.

The mansion had once belonged to the Deluca family, a venerable and affluent family of Tuscan descent who had migrated to America seeking opportunity and traveled west seeking gold. As they were a moneyed family, the mansion became a place of social consequence, frequented by the area's dignitaries—the politicians and merchants who ran the territory. The family remained in the home for only two generations, when they moved on to California and the manufacture of repeating rifles, finding more gold in war than mines. The estate was purchased by then mayor Ardell Carnahan, who occupied its opulent halls until 1876, when he fled the town after embezzling a sizable amount of money from the city coffers. The mansion was purchased from the city and became the Arcadia Paradise Inn until 1929, when the Ogden Canyon trolley ceased its operations and the inn fell into bankruptcy. The home was boarded up and sat vacant until it was discovered by transients and became a flophouse. It was not peaceful then, for men fought for the possession of a home they did not own, and at least two men were killed under its roof, seeking only its shelter.

Six years later the estate was purchased by an eccentric Austrian man, who lived on the second floor of the house and used the main floor for livestock. Swine and asses dined where politicians once had, and this he found fitting. The man's hermitry was successful; when he died of natural causes, he and his animals were not found until a year later by trespassing hikers.

The property was acquired by the county for tax delinquency and used to house machinery for canyon maintenance up until 1973, when with the stroke of a pen, the home was designated as a rest home for the elderly.

With bureaucratic zeal, the home was institutionalized—carved rosewood bookshelves were removed to accommodate sheet-metal filing cabinets; high coffered ceilings were concealed beneath hung ceiling tile, while bolts of thin industrial carpet smothered polished wooden floors and parquets. Still, the mansion's core beauty—born of craftsmen who left a portion of their soul with each gouge of a wood chisel or scribe of a marking knife—could not be silenced.

When I arrived at work a few days later, dawn rolled across the Arcadia in a thin fog, settling in the terraced cliffs of the canyon and pouring out into the valley like a tributary into a vast sea. I was met on arrival by Helen near the front entryway. She was pulling on a fur-lined parka.

"Are you leaving?"

She nodded. "I was just waiting for you. I need you to drive Henri to the veterans hos-

pital. His bronchitis isn't getting any better."
She looked at my car. "You better take the
van. I'll get the keys." I followed her back to
her office.

"Where are you off to?"

"Some fool bureaucrat wants our building
for a new children's day care. I don't know
why we're always the first neck on the chop-
ping block. As if I didn't have enough to do
without wasting my time justifying our existence. I have a friend in the commissioner's
office who's agreed to help us out. I'm meeting with her to get advice."

She handed me the keys. "Do you know
where you're going?"

"Veterans hospital, down off Wall Avenue."

"The hospital should already have his
Medicaid record. Just wait there until he's
through, unless they want to keep him
overnight. Any questions?"

"Who's Henri?"

"He's in room six on the second floor. He's
the black man with the amputation."

"I'll get right to him."

Henri's room was a study in the tao of yin
and yang. He shared the room with another
man, and though their quarters were sepa-

rated only by a sheer cloth curtain hung from an aluminum ceiling track, they were a world apart. Henri's roommate was an Asian man with long gray hair and a scraggly beard. He was called simply Chen, his family surname, as all had long given up trying to pronounce or remember the second two syllables of his name. Chen had adorned his room as eclectically as a Chinese shrine, with golden Buddhas and dragon-shaped incense trays, pungent even when not lit. Next to his bed was a large cloisonné vase in the shape of a chicken. Red pennants of golden Chinese characters hung from the wall next to ink color paintings of bamboo and the Guangzhou countryside. In contrast to his roommate's, Henri's space was austere, without a single photograph or keepsake, except for a single cardboard box about the size of a pencil case. It had sat next to his bed unopened since he came to the Arcadia, and no one knew what it contained, or cared enough to ask.

I found Henri lying in bed, turned toward the wall, his sheets pulled tightly around himself. He was fully dressed and his forehead was beaded with fever.

"Henri, I'm here to take you to the hospital," I said. He lay still for a moment, then erupted in another fit of coughing. Without further prompting, he pushed himself up by one arm, then slid his leg over the bed's edge, grabbed his crutch, and hobbled ahead of me out to the elevator.

The drive to the hospital was silent except for a brief and futile attempt at conversation. A mile from the home I asked casually, "Been at the Arcadia for a while?"

Henri did not reply but began to cough, partially covering his mouth with his hand.

"That cough sounds like it hurts. How long have you had it?"

Still no response.

"Alice says you do a song-and-dance routine in the dayroom on Friday nights."

He turned away and I drove on in silence, regretting the remark.

The veterans hospital was a squat, yellow-bricked building with mold-green tiled floors and pocked, eggshell white ceiling tiles. After I waded through the requisite admissions papers, a nurse led Henri away and I sat down in the lobby with a magazine. Not long after, the nurse returned for me.

"Are you the one who brought the gentleman from the nursing home?"

"Yes."

"Dr. Heath would like to see you."

I followed the nurse back to a room where Henri sat on a vinyl examination table, wearing only a thin cotton gown tied at the back. He looked frail and small. His crutch lay against the wall and his eyes darted about anxiously, as if he were about to bolt. The doctor sat next to him on a tan Naugahyde stool, writing at a clipboard. At my entrance, he adjusted his glasses as he rotated toward me.

"Did this man have a fall?"

I looked over at Henri, who did not acknowledge the query. "I don't know. I was only told that he had bronchitis."

"Look at this." He lifted the side of Henri's gown, exposing several large bruises and bandages on his ribs and hips. The black skin was almost purple where the doctor had rubbed iodine across the wounds, covering them with pads of gauze held in place by white strips of medical adhesive.

"Are they bedsores?"

"No. They're abrasions. It appears that he fell against something. I noticed he came in with just a single crutch; it may be that he needs a wheelchair."

"We check daily for bedsores," I said. "I'm surprised this wasn't noticed. I could have the director call you."

The doctor returned to his clipboard. "That won't be necessary. I just wanted to bring this to your attention." He finished his scrawling, then handed me several notes inscribed with cryptic markings. "Does he have his own room?"

"He shares with another man."

"I recommend moving one of them out. Bronchial pneumonia can be fatal. Especially for the geriatric. I've put him on a stronger antibiotic than what he's been on. Make sure he takes it four times daily on a full stomach. This other prescription is for his cough. It will make him drowsy. Is he on any other medications?"

"I don't know. But I can check when I get back."

"Call if he is."

I helped Henri back to the van, and the only sound of the ride was the din of the traffic and Henri's sporadic bursts of coughing. The fog had mostly lifted, and I parked the van near the front door and helped Henri down. Without a word, Henri grabbed his crutch and hobbled off, having little desire for my further assistance or company. I locked the van, then followed him into the Arcadia. Inside the entryway Alice sat at the front desk working a crossword puzzle. I set the prescriptions on the counter in front of her.

"How do I get prescriptions filled?"

"That's my job. I take care of all medications."

"I need to get these filled for Henri as soon as possible. Is he on any other medications?"

"No," Alice replied.

I returned the keys to Helen's office and grabbed the newspaper for Esther. By the time I reemerged, Alice already had medicine bottles in hand.

"I've got Henri's medicine right here. We had leftover."

"Leftovers? Aren't medications supposed to be used until they're gone?"

Alice set both bottles on the countertop. "Not if the patient croaks."

I was taken aback by her response. "Well, I guess there's no sense letting them go to waste," I said. I took the medicine and climbed the stairs to Henri's room. The room's lights were off and the drawn blinds glowed amber, backlit from the afternoon sun. Henri had recocooned himself in his sheets, though his eyes were open and followed me as I entered the room. I retrieved a cup from his bathroom, filled it with tap water, then poured the thick syrup into a spoon.

"I brought your medicine, Henri."

He slowly raised himself, his eyes following the spoon and its burgundy medicine. I sat down next to his bed and held the spoon up to his mouth. Suddenly his arm flailed out, knocking both the spoon and glass from my hand. The glass shattered against the floor. He began groaning and writhing in wild contortions. His gaze was fixed on the doorway. I turned back to see Alice standing in the threshold, looking in. She was shaking her head.

"Is this an epileptic seizure?"

"No, he's just senile," she said. "That's why he's not recovering; he won't take his medicine." She again shook her head. "Good luck."

She returned downstairs. I rubbed the old man's shoulder and he seemed to calm. "It's okay, Henri. I'm just going to clean this up. We'll try again later."

I retrieved a broom and swept up the glass, then mopped up the floor. By the time I had finished, Henri had fallen asleep.

chapter four

La Caille

"Today a man was shot in Betheltown. While murder is commonplace in Goldstrike, this is the first of such incidents in Betheltown. The dispute was over an abandoned claim of the Layola mine. . . . Money is a cheap way to sell one's soul."

Excerpt from Esther Huish's Diary

I clocked out that evening at six o'clock, changed into a shirt and necktie, and made the hour drive to Salt Lake City to meet Faye at her friend's wedding.

A by-product of my association with Faye was to be brought into contact with many things that were previously unexperienced—a more affluent slice of the American pie—and La Caille was one of them. I entered the restaurant's massive château gates after dark. The snowbanked cobblestone driveway was lit by the soft amber glow of kerosene sconces with etched-glass hurricane lanterns, held aloft by long thin poles tied with chiffon ribbon. The snow was spread smooth like icing over the spacious yard, and I had heard that reindeer, llamas, emus, and peacocks roamed the restaurant's grounds in the warmer months of the year. At the end of the long driveway was a turnaround where a valet traded my car keys for a claim ticket. I went inside.

When I first met Faye I was given to anxiety attacks in such places of sophistication, but exposure had somewhat dulled their edges, and I learned to look like I belonged. At least I thought I did.

I checked my coat inside the doorway, then climbed the tapestry-lined circular stairwell upstairs to the main floor, where the wedding dinner had already commenced. The bride and groom had been announced for dinner, followed by a champagne toast and the distribution of menus. The wedding ceremony had taken place an hour earlier, and a string ensemble now occupied the garden room where vows had been exchanged. A large, six-tiered alabaster wedding cake strewn with fresh flowers was displayed on a round linen-covered table near the center of the dining room, surrounded by four silver candelabra.

At the far end of the room, Faye sat at the head table next to the bride's mother, dressed in a pleated cream silk blouse with a cowl neckline, tied at the waist with a sash of like material. The head table had already been served, and Faye was delicately dissecting a puff pastry when she saw me. Her face lit as she rose to greet me.

"Hello, handsome. You look great," she said, taking my hand.

"I've been told that I clean up real nice." I glanced down at those sitting with her. Shandra sat close to her new husband—a tall dark-haired man dressed in charcoal gray tails.

"You've broken with decorum," I whispered to Faye. "The bridesmaid's not supposed to be more beautiful than the bride."

Faye slightly blushed, then glanced back at the table. "Shhh," she said happily. "Don't say that. I'm not." She stepped behind me. "I need to make introductions."

Shandra gazed up at us, smiling. I knew Shandra from several previous occasions and she had been with Faye the day we first met, at Heller's.

"Michael, meet Mrs. Millett."

"You look beautiful, Shandra."

Her smile spread still broader. "Thank you. I'm so happy you could come. I'm glad you finally get to meet Tim." She took her groom's hand and he left his conversation midsentence and glanced up at me. "Michael, this is my new husband. Tim, this is Faye's beau."

The groom smiled and extended his hand. "It's a pleasure to finally meet you, Michael. Faye has said much about you."

"As she has about you," I replied. "Congratulations. I adore your wife."

"Not too much, I hope," he said, smiling.

Shandra then introduced me to her parents. "Mom, Dad, this is Michael, Faye's boyfriend."

Shandra's mother was a refined woman with sharp features and dark tinted hair pulled back tightly in an immaculate French knot—a style in contrast to her husband, who was a large hirsute man with bushy silver-laced eyebrows and a projecting jaw. I could imagine him in a bolo tie and ostrich-skin boots. The man smiled, exaggerating his crow's-feet.

"It is a pleasure making your acquaintance," the woman cordially enunciated.

"It's a pleasure, Michael," the man said

brashly. "Now, why don't we have you sitting with us?" He looked over the crowded bridal table. "Just drag a chair on over."

Shandra looked slightly uncomfortable. "I'm sorry . . ."

I quickly raised my hand. "Oh no, sir, it's quite all right. I already have a seat over here," I said, vaguely gesturing to the dining room. "I just wanted to check on my girl before someone else claimed her."

The man laughed. "Well, I was thinking of claiming her myself," he said jovially. He leaned toward me. "She's kinda easy on the eyes."

I liked this man. He was not so much out of place in these surroundings as they were out of place with him.

"I couldn't agree more. Again, congratulations to you all," I said, stepping away from the table.

Faye stepped back with me. "You handled that well," she whispered.

"Where do I sit?"

"They have you seated at table seven. It's the one by the large window."

I espied a table across the room with a vacant seat.

"I'm really sorry, I thought they would have

us sitting together," Faye apologized. "I didn't know the bridesmaids were at the head table."

"I'll be fine," I assured her. "Just enjoy yourself."

"I'll be over as soon as I can."

She still looked concerned, so I changed the subject.

"Has everything gone well today?"

She looked at me dreamily. "It's been a fairy tale. Shandra is so happy."

"You're getting ideas, aren't you?"

She smiled and did not answer.

"Well, I'll just hang out over at table seven until you're finished."

"I won't be long," she promised. Her eyebrows raised slightly and she said joyfully, "There's dancing downstairs." I started to leave when a mischievous smile crossed her face and she said, "Remind me to tell you about the champagne incident."

I crossed the room and sat down at the only available seat left at the table. At the setting, there was a silver-framed place card with my scripted name. The dinnerware was set around a tall crystal-vase centerpiece with flowers matching the bride's bouquet. I nodded to the other guests as I sat, though they were already immersed in conversation and only vaguely noticed my arrival.

A waitress clad in a low-cut bustier with a tight laced waist and blousy French sleeves came to my side. "You decided to come?" she teased. She carried a carafe of red wine. "Would you like some wine?"

"No, thank you. But I would like some dinner."

"We have two choices of entrées, rack of lamb or charbroiled halibut."

"I'll have the lamb."

She nodded. "For dessert we have Venetian trifle and crepe maison."

"The crepe sounds good."

"Would you like that served flambée?"

I looked at her quizzically. "I'm sorry, I don't know what that means."

The waitress smiled. "It means we light it on fire."

The elfin man sitting directly across from me leaned over and whispered to his companion. She glanced at me.

I ignored the exchange. "That will be fine. Thank you."

I lifted a croissant and buttered it as I surveyed the table's occupants. There were two well-dressed middle-aged couples, one of whom had consumed too much of the wine and the other of whom looked as though they needed more. Sandwiched between the couples was a sanguine elderly woman with silver hair and an enormous amethyst broach. To my left were three young women: a tall slim blonde sat in the middle, flanked by a pout-faced blonde with dark roots and a black velvet choker, and a redheaded girl with narrow glasses set upon a sharp small nose. All three were attired in gowns of obvious expense and picked daintily at their plates as if more interested in redesigning the food than eating it. Though they were all likely still in their teens, they spoke urbanely, like women twice their age.

"The gown's to die for, but she should have passed on the jeweled-tiara thing. I think it's gauche."

"I think Shandra has better taste in clothing than in men," said the redhead.

"All women have better taste in clothing than in men," the slim blonde replied. "It's easier to pick clothes than men."

"The problem with men is that you only get to pick once and then pray he stays in fashion the rest of your life."

The slim blonde laughed. "Who says you only get to pick once?"

"I don't know what your problem is," said the redhead indignantly. "He's handsome and his father owns half of Park City, which makes him twice as handsome."

The pseudo blonde poked at her food with a silver fork. "What's with this baked Brie? It's like, Brie became haute cuisine, so they put it in everything. They'll probably have Brie cheesecake for dessert."

"Flambée," the slim blonde said, laughing, and I wondered if it was in reference to my exchange with the waitress.

"Who's the bridesmaid with the cute auburn hair?" asked the redhead.

"That's Faye," said the slim blonde. "She's a Sigma."

"Faye's a sweetheart," said the pseudo blonde. "We pledged together. She's premed."

"Everyone says they're premed," said the redhead.

"Faye's not just smoke. She's a chemistry major and her father's a neurosurgeon. She's a brain."

"I'd rather die than think that much," said the slim blonde.

"At least she won't have to worry about who she marries," said the redhead.

"You make it sound like she's going to marry a bricklayer," said the pseudo blonde.

"I just mean she can marry someone nice."

"'Nice' doesn't pay down Neiman Marcus," the slim blonde postulated. "Or dress like it could. I mean, what if you get tired of the workingwoman bit?"

"Aren't you the romantic," the redhead said sarcastically.

"I'm realistic. The poor-boy thing is great for soap operas, but slumming doesn't hold water in the real world. You either wise up or end up in a bowling league." She lifted her glass. "It's a phase every woman goes through sooner or later—it's a Cinderella fantasy in reverse. Doesn't work. I say, marry rich."

"Marry rich and often," added the pseudo blonde.

"I give them three years," the slim blonde said, looking toward the head table. "Five if he never gets caught."

The redhead laughed. "They shouldn't allow you near a wedding. You're a bad omen."

"A wedding is a bad omen," she replied cavalierly. "Like, you're some Pollyanna."

"Did you see Chris downstairs?" the pseudo blonde interjected.

"Chris Haight is here?" asked the red-head.

The three women abruptly left the table. A few minutes later the waitress returned with my dinner, and I ate slowly as the other guests finished their meals and departed. Faye came over as I was finishing.

"Anyone sitting here?"

"No. She went to find Chris."

Faye sat down. "Sorry that took so long." She looked at my dessert. "I love crepe flambée. May I have a bite?"

I pushed my plate toward her. "Tell me about the champagne incident."

Faye's face lit with amusement. "It's humorous now, but it wasn't earlier. Tim's father brought more than six dozen bottles of champagne. The restaurant ran out of room in their refrigerator so one of the managers told a busboy to take a clean garbage can and fill it with ice to chill the champagne. He came back an hour later to find the busboy pouring the last case into the garbage can."

She shook her head, laughing. "Can you imagine?"

"I can imagine myself doing something like that."

Faye took my hand. "Let's go dance."

We danced until the bride and groom cut the wedding cake and threw the bouquet, which Faye caught, though the ritual had clearly been rigged as Shandra all but handed it to her. Shandra and Tim made their departure and the ecologically minded crowd threw birdseed as the couple departed. The wedding had been planned to the nth detail, and doves were released as the newlyweds climbed into the white stretch limousine that awaited them. They had planned to release butterflies instead, shipped in from a mail order company in California, but the insects died in the shipping.

As we made the long drive home, I reflected again on the dinner conversation. As easily as I had dismissed the young women, on a deeper level I found their observations disturbing. The notion that I was a phase that all women pass through did not sit well with me, and even though Faye utterly lacked pretentiousness, they were, like Faye, products of the same society. I couldn't help but wonder at what level Faye shared their opinions or had considered their notions of Cinderella fantasies and bowling leagues. While I ruminated over these things, Faye laid her head on my shoulder.

"Is something troubling you?"

"Why do you ask?"

"You've been more quiet than usual."

"Weddings have that effect on men."

She grinned. "I'm sorry I'm not better company. I'm just so tired."

"Did you even sleep last night?"

"Just a few hours. But today's been nice." She closed her eyes and a smile of contentment blanketed her face. "It was everything a wedding should be."

chapter five

Faye's
Acceptance

"Betheltown is dying. Only the Salisbury mine remains, but it too will soon close. Only a few of us remain to die with the town. I suppose that I should not wonder at my present circumstance. That which we expect of life is indeed all that it ever can be."

Excerpt from Esther Huish's Diary

I am not one to hang much credence on first impressions, as it is my experience that the initial impression we accept of others is usually as flawed as the one we seek to project. I found this true not only of Esther, but of nearly every coworker at the Arcadia as well. My position as a nurse's aide required certification, which obliged me for a time to follow a more experienced coworker, Sharon, on her daily rounds. Sharon was a tall brunette woman who wore narrow rectangular eyeglasses like the reading spectacles sold on plastic racks at the supermarket. She hailed from a small town in northern Utah that I had never heard of, despite the fact that it was within a half hour's drive from Ogden. She was reserved and somber, which I initially mistook for petulance. In truth she was gentle and kind, and Helen's maxim about those with the softest hearts applied to Sharon as well as it did to Esther. To this day I think of Sharon fondly.

Though I worked mostly at Sharon's side, each day was busier than the previous one, as Helen increased my responsibilities as quickly as I mastered them. The one duty I had not yet been assigned was to walk Esther, and though I saw the woman each day when changing her bedding, she would sit quietly in her chair dozing whenever I entered, though I suspect that at least twice she was feigning sleep to avoid the unlikely possibility of another tête-à-tête.

It had snowed three more inches before dawn on Monday, and the morning traffic slowed to match the precarious road conditions. Consequently I arrived at work a few minutes tardy. Alice stood next to the time clock, brushing the snow from her coat and examining the newly posted December work schedules on the bulletin board.

"I thought you worked nights this week," I said.

"I just came in to pick up my check. Damn that heifer."

I glanced over at her. "What heifer?"

"Helen's got me scheduled late on Christmas Eve."

I hung my coat in my locker. "You had other plans?"

"I was invited to a Christmas Eve party in Park City. Night skiing, boys, and beer."

"Sounds decadent for Christmas."

"That's the best kind of Christmas."

I checked my own schedule. "I could work for you."

The offer surprised her. "You would do that?"

"I don't have anything planned for Christmas Eve."

Alice immediately picked up the phone and dialed. "I owe you, Michael." She cradled the phone against her shoulder. "Too bad I can't bring you with me. The girls would think I finally traded up."

"Just happy to contribute to your delinquency."

"I'll make it up to you sometime."

* * *

Around noon the county health department nurses arrived to administer flu shots to the Arcadia residents, whom the staff herded like cattle to branding irons. It was the first time that I saw Esther leave her room, and I took advantage of the chance to work in her absence. As I was finishing changing her bedding, I noticed something lying on the floor across the room. Something metallic. I lifted it carefully in my palm. It was a small silver-plated locket, old and intricately engraved with delicate flourishes and florals that exposed pale gold where the silver had begun to wear. From a distance it appeared to be of sterling silver, but as I examined it more closely, I discovered it to have only been coated in the white metal, which concealed the more precious metal beneath. Across the back of the piece, inscribed in diminutive script, were two words: *Always, Thomas.*I pried the locket apart to expose two small photographs—a hand-tinted photograph of a young, nubile woman, fresh faced and slender with high cheeks and dark haunting eyes, opposite an aged, sepia-hued photograph of a young man with wire-rimmed glasses and cinnamon hair tossed and careless, his face struck in youthful confidence.

The chain's clasp was slightly bowed, which I concluded had caused its fall from the old woman's neck, so I bent the clasp back into place before laying the locket on the bureau. I went back to my chores without giving the piece a second thought.

That evening, as I descended the stairs at the end of my shift, Faye was waiting for me on a vinyl chair next to the front counter. She was talking with Alice but stopped to greet me.

"Hello, handsome."

I smiled, surprised to see her. "What are you doing here?"

"I wanted to see where my boyfriend works."

Alice turned back to her work.

Faye stood, her face lit with excitement. "The real reason is that I've got exciting news. I've been accepted to Johns Hopkins!"

"Congratulations," I said, embracing her. "I knew you would."

"I still can't believe it."

Faye was in her final year of premed at

Weber State College, and after a stellar MCAT exam had begun applying to medical schools. Johns Hopkins was her dream—a prayer tossed from behind the three-point line.

"My father is so proud."

"I would think so. Next fall his little girl's a med student."

Unexpectedly, Faye's countenance fell. She held my hands as she stepped back. "That's the bad news."

"There's bad news to this?"

She hesitated. "Weber doesn't offer three of the courses I need to graduate by next fall. I am going to have to finish my bachelor's at Johns Hopkins."

"When?"

"Winter quarter. Class starts January fifth. Dad and I are flying to Baltimore in a couple of weeks to look for housing." She looked at me apologetically. "It's the only way I will graduate by next fall."

I was stunned. It was this part of Faye's dream that we had both anticipated with thinly veiled dread, as it would put two thousand miles between us. Over the past year I placated myself with the reminder that it was still a long way off.

"That only gives us a little over a month."

She looked suddenly sad. I did not want to diminish the excitement of her accomplishment, so I put my arms back around her. "It's okay. We'll make the most of it."

chapter six

Thanksgiving

"There are those who, in the same breath, pray for the poor and for the blessing of never encountering them."

Excerpt from Esther Huish's Diary

Faye's father, Dr. Benjamin Murrow, NSR, was a man of decorum, which means he was more likely to spread his hostility with a butter knife than a butcher's. He was tall and thick boned, with dark brown hair impeccably oiled and combed back like a prep student of the fifties. There was a nervous formality to his demeanor—he was the kind of man who introduced himself as "Doctor" and wore a necktie to dinner in his own home.

He was an accomplished surgeon and an assertive patriarch who pushed his children according to a script indelibly etched in his mind. A script I had no part in. Ballet and tumbling, piano lessons, swimming lessons at the country club, and honor students all. While I was happy that Faye had been blessed with these opportunities, they still served as another evidence of the distance between our upbringings. Faye's mother, Virginia—Ginny to the girls—was a beautiful woman with a luxuriant Southern accent and even more luxuriant charm, the kind of prize one picks up at a debutante ball. Mrs. Murrow held no disregard for me, but she too had come from a regimented home and kept her opinions to herself, though at times I'd see sympathy in her eyes and I guess that made her a silent ally. Faye had two younger sisters, Jayne, a junior in high school, and Abigail, who was a freshman. Like Faye, they were bright and spontaneous, and it was hard to believe such spirits were a product of so rigid a home.

It was not the first time I had been to Faye's for dinner—a verbal gauntlet that I endured for the sake of Faye and her faith in her father's conversion: that if he could not bless our courtship, he might, at least, relax his opposition. But it seemed clear to everyone but Faye that things were moving inversely, and each new encounter with her father further steeled his determination to effect my disappearance from his daughter's life.

The home was filled with Thanksgiving smells as we gathered at the lace-clothed table. This was my first Thanksgiving without my mother, and I had never, outside the pages of a magazine, witnessed such a feast, let alone sat down to one. The table was arrayed with brimming bowls of steaming succotash and turnips, paprika-dusted mashed potatoes with giblet gravy, Parker House rolls, bread dressing, candied yams, cranberry sauce, and a large china platter of basted turkey. The cuisine was the highlight of an otherwise dismal experience, and I hoped to get well into the meal before the inevitable haranguing began. Only a few bites after the doctor thanked God for the bounty with which they had been blessed, he started in on me for my lack of such things.

"Faye tells us you have a new job."

I wiped my mouth with a napkin. "Yes, sir. At a nursing care facility."

"So, you have already abdicated higher education?"

"No, sir. I'm not in school. I have been paying off bills and saving for tuition."

"Aren't there grants for people like you?"

Faye glared at him.

"There are grants for lower-income students, but I've applied for an academic scholarship."

"Michael is a finalist for the president's scholarship," Faye interjected proudly. "He had a three-eight average his first year."

The doctor was unimpressed. "So, what is your responsibility at this facility? Changing bedpans?"

"Among other things."

He then said to Faye, as if I weren't present, "You know that Fred Hobson was accepted to Stanford's MBA program. I ran into his father at the club. Good family, the Hobsons."

"Fred's a sociopath," Faye said bluntly. "I'm glad he's out of state. I'll sleep better at night."

Dr. Murrow glared at me, assuming I was the root of such insolence. "You know Faye has been accepted to Johns Hopkins?" he said to me.

"Of course he knows," Faye said.

"Baltimore is a long ways away," the doctor shared with great pleasure, as if he had forgotten that he too would be deprived of Faye's presence.

"I think Faye and Michael should just get married and move to Baltimore together," Abigail said abruptly. There was a stunned silence, and Mrs. Murrow anxiously glanced to her husband. Dr. Murrow was dumbstruck and his face bent in pain. I wondered if Abigail had said this because she meant it or because she was sure that it would silence her father. Either way, we finished the meal in silence. After dinner Faye and I donned our coats and, carrying plates of pumpkin pie, walked through the crusted snow to the back of the Tudor home, sitting close to each other in the gazebo swing. The dusk shimmered in light wisps of snowfall as the temperature fell with the sun. Inside the house someone began to play on the home's ebony grand piano.

"I'm sorry, Michael. I don't know what gets into him."

"He just thinks he's protecting you from the enemy."

"He doesn't know who his enemies are." She leaned into me and I put my arm around her.

"I know it's a ways off and this isn't the best time to ask, but I wanted to invite you to spend Christmas Eve with us."

"I couldn't do that. It wouldn't be fair to your family."

"Then I'll spend it with you."

I kissed her forehead. "I've already promised Alice that I would work late for her on Christmas Eve."

"Why did you do that?"

"I didn't have any other plans and I didn't want to be alone. This will be my first Christmas without family."

Faye took my hand. "I would have spent it with you."

"I know you would have. That's why I committed myself. You should be with your family. This may be your last Christmas at home."

Faye read into the comment and smiled.

"Well, we still have Christmas Day together."

"From dawn to dusk," I said.

She sighed. "There is so much to do before then. When do you meet with the scholarship board?"

"Next Wednesday."

"That's what I thought. I'm sorry that I won't be there for you. I'll be in Baltimore looking for housing." She smiled. "But you'll charm them."

"I don't think the scholarship committee consists of people who like to be charmed. When do you get back?"

"Friday." She looked down, suddenly reflective. "I don't know what I will do without you at school."

"I just wonder how long it will take for you to forget about me," I quipped. It was a coping mechanism I had long before perfected, relegating my greatest fears to flippancy. Faye became suddenly solemn.

"Why is it so hard for you to believe in my love?"

I looked into her eyes. "Because you're contrary to everything in my life. You're like a mirage. It's hard for me to believe that someone as bright and beautiful as you isn't going to just disappear when I get near."

"What proof would you have of my love?"

"I'm not looking for proof."

"Yes, you are. Name it. Ask for a commitment."

"I don't need a commitment."

She set down her plate and laid her head on my shoulder. "What did you think of Abigail's comment?"

"I thought your father would have a stroke."

She smiled. "I know what he thought. What did you think?"

The earnestness of her query surprised me. "Marrying you would be like winning the lottery—one of those good things that happen to other people. I've always assumed it was just somewhere off the horizon. It seems that's where good things always lie."

Faye smiled sweetly. "I know we're young, Michael, but I think I'm ready. My parents would have me wait until everything in my life is neat and tidy with hospital corners. But life isn't best lived that way. I see couples who have built their lives together, struggling through the hard times. Some say it's the best years of their lives. I want that. I don't want some by-the-book life with neatly penned entrances like it were a Broadway production. I want to live it. For better or worse." She kissed me on the cheek. "I love you, Michael. You're what I've always wanted."

"A poor, uneducated adult orphan with a wretched past?" I asked sarcastically.

She grinned. "... with a heart of gold." She wove her fingers through mine. "Will you think about it, Michael?"

chapter seven

The Committee

"Today a group of miners organized to bar negroes from working in the mines. The greatest evils of this world have always been performed by committee."

Excerpt from Esther Huish's Diary

Faye and her father flew out for Baltimore Monday afternoon. At her request I did not see her off and we said our good-byes the previous evening. We had spent the whole of Sunday together, attending the local parish with her family, which I had happily discovered was a sanctuary of sorts from Dr. Murrow's assaults. After the service we came back to my home and made dinner, and then spent the afternoon on the couch saying good-bye, relishing the bittersweet sentiments of separation. Tuesday night Faye called from Baltimore to wish me luck on my scholarship interview.

In truth, the scholarship had more to do with my mental state than my fiscal one. As Dr. Murrow had tactfully pointed out, "people like me" qualified for financial aid. I suspect that I was looking for validation—someone outside of my own dreams to tell me that I somehow belonged at the institution. I think I wanted it most of all for Faye. Not that she required it, but she deserved it.

I had arranged to work only the last half of the day on Wednesday, and I arrived early that morning at the university. Seated with me in the reception room were the other students against whom I vied for the scholarship. With the exception of the palpable anxiety, it was a morgue of a room, anemic and solemn, with bodies shuffled in and out with quiet efficiency. Twenty minutes after my arrival a middle-aged blonde woman in a polyester business suit emerged from the doorway to call out my name. I followed her into the conference room—a broad and grim chamber with dark wood paneling and thick-framed oil paintings of former university presidents robed in the vestments of their office.

At the woman's instruction I sat alone at the end of a mahogany conference table opposite the four men and three women who had already commenced their scrutiny. She proceeded to present me to the committee.

"Our next finalist is Michael Keddington. Michael maintained a three-point-five grade point average in high school, which increased his freshman year in college to a three-point-eight-seven, exceeding our minimum scholarship criteria. He also has demonstrated financial need, which, of course, is only relevant in the case of a tie among candidates. His application was made directly to the educational board instead of the board of regents because he has already had one year of higher education. Michael dropped out of college after his freshman year but is now ready to return to complete his degree as a fully matriculated student. He plans to pursue an undergraduate degree in education."

The man at the head of the table—a collegiate-looking man with a receding hairline, a tweed jacket, and wire-rimmed glasses—cleared his throat. There was a stack of papers in front of him next to a hand-thrown glazed coffee cup.

"I am Craig Scott, dean of the College of Education and chairman of this scholarship board. Michael, this committee has already reviewed and discussed your candidacy and we have a few concerns. You are clearly a good student. Your transcripts are impressive and your written essay was superior. However, your community involvement and extracurricular activities are well below our expectations—so far below that had you not so excelled academically, your candidacy would not now be under consideration. The presidential scholarship is one of this university's most prestigious. We expect and demand that our applicants are active participants in bettering not only the academic community, but the communities in which they live. To be candid, we are hoping that there is some involvement that you have not included on your application."

My heart sank.

"No, sir. I wish that there were."

"Could you please explain to this committee why you have such minimal extracurricular involvement?"

I took a deep breath. "It is not that I haven't interest in community affairs. I just haven't had the kind of . . . background that lent itself to such activities."

He gazed pointedly at me. "Please elaborate."

I had hoped to keep my personal background from being drawn out. "Ever since I was fifteen I've had to work after school to help provide for my family. For the past two years my mother's health deteriorated to the point that all I did was care for her. My first year in college I enrolled in leadership with several service clubs, but I wasn't ever able to be as active as I should have been, so I didn't feel right in including those organizations on my application."

Suddenly another man spoke.

"I am Professor William Doxey of the College of Communications. I have an even greater concern with your candidacy than the objection just stated. By acceptance of this scholarship you may, in fact, deny another student an important opportunity to receive an education. As this is the case, what assurance does this committee have that you will not drop out of school again?"

"I give you my word."

He smiled condescendingly. "Of course, we would all hope to believe that, but as the trustees of this endowment, how can we truly be certain of your intentions?"

I gazed silently at the row of stoic faces awaiting an answer. I felt angry that I had to continually justify the time spent caring for my mother, as if it were somehow less worthy than the deeds performed by service clubs that did little more than provide venues for ongoing parties. The greatest acts of altruism have always been performed without audience or plaques.

"Well, my mother can't die again."

The man stared back blankly while several of his colleagues grinned. A wry smile crossed the face of the dean, and he glanced from side to side. "Are there any more questions for Mr. Keddington?"

Receiving no response, he turned back to me. "Thank you, Michael. Is there anything you would like to say to this committee before you leave?"

I stood up. "I just want to say thank you for this opportunity. I don't believe life owes us anything but that."

As I was ushered out of the room, Professor Doxey smiled. That night I called Faye in Baltimore to report. Characteristically, she was certain I would get it.

* * *

The following noon, Alice walked into the employees' break room as I sat down to a cafeteria tray.

"I thought you were off today," I said.

"I came to take you to lunch."

I glanced down at the meal—pressed chicken cloaked beneath a pale yellow gelatinous sauce. "And waste this?"

"If you're attached to it, you can bring it with you."

"What's the occasion?" I asked, standing.

"I'm thanking you in advance for working for me on Christmas Eve."

"I'll just dispose of this," I said, taking the tray to the cafeteria.

At the base of Ogden Canyon is a quaint emporium with one of the city's better kitchens. It is a chimera of a place, part shop, part eatery, but eclectic in the right measure, and Faye and I had dined there at least a half dozen times previously, though the best visits are during the holidays, when the estate is dressed in its most festive adornment. I learned that it was one of Alice's regular stops when the waitress asked her if she wanted the usual before she took my order. When she had delivered our meals, Alice sat back poking at a Chinese chicken salad.

"Are you working tonight?" she asked.

"I'm pulling another double."

"I don't know how you do it."

"It's easy when you're broke."

"Well, you'll never get rich working there." She took a bite of salad. "What do you think of working in a rest home?"

"It's taken me a little while to get used to it."

"It took me a year to get used to it and a month to get sick of it," Alice said cynically. "Old people drive me crazy."

"Then why are you working there?"

"My father."

I looked at her quizzically. "Your father is in the center?"

She laughed. "No. You don't know who my father is?"

I shook my head. "I have no idea."

"Starley Richards . . . head of the state Division of Human Services."

I had heard the name. "He's your father?"

"He's priming me for a director's role."

"Like Helen's."

She grimaced at the comparison. "In a manner of speaking."

"Why would you want her job?"

"It's not a bad job. At least it's at the top of the food chain."

"I wondered how it was that you got along so poorly with Helen."

"Nepotism. She can't fire me, and it drives her nuts. Dad is her boss's boss's boss." She brushed her hair back from her face, eager to change the topic. "I haven't seen your girlfriend for a while."

"She's out of town. She went back east to look for housing."

"That's right, Johns Hopkins. Baltimore is a long ways away."

"So I've been reminded."

"How long have the two of you been together?"

"We met last summer."

"Then you're still in the honeymoon phase. She's gorgeous."

"I think so."

"But she's not your type."

"Gorgeous isn't my type?"

"No, you're gorgeous too. I mean, a preppy little princess. There's more denim to you than silk."

"Spoken from a Levi's dweller."

"If the pants fit . . ."

I smiled, amused by our banter. "I suppose that's part of our problem. We've talked about marriage, but there are some real differences in our backgrounds. I couldn't possibly give her the life she's accustomed to. Frankly, I don't know if I'm protecting her from a more difficult life or if I'm protecting myself from when she decides she can't take it anymore and leaves."

Alice nodded as if she understood.

"What about you? You must have more than a few men in your life."

"A dozen or so," she squibbed. "They're just for fun. Last month one of them actually asked me to marry him."

"What did you say?"

"I told him to get real."

"You are a charmer."

She laughed at herself. "Life is too short. Live hard, die young, leave nothing. I'll tell you this much. I'd rather be impaled than end up living in a nursing home." She leaned forward over her salad. "You know what old people talk about all day? Bowel movements and feet. When you're young you don't give either a second thought, but as soon as you get gray hair they're big

news. The day I talk about a bowel movement in public is the day I slit my wrists."

I grinned.

"I mean, you could end up like that
recluse on the third floor."

"You mean Esther?"

She waved her hand. "The woman's a nut-
case. She just sits in her room all day and
cries."

"Do you know what's wrong with her?"

"Dementia."

"She didn't seem demented when I spoke
with her."

"She actually spoke to you?"

"My first day at work."

"I've been here three years now and I
don't think she's said two words. She talks to
Helen sometimes, but I assumed it was because they're both bizarre."

I did not care for her assessment of Helen. I glanced down at my watch, then
downed my Coke. "I better get back."

Unhurried, Alice took her lipstick from her
purse and carefully applied it, looking into a
compact mirror. "We should do this again
sometime." She snapped shut her compact,
then lifted our meal tab. "Next time I'll let you
take me."

* * *

That evening I was carrying dinner to Esther's room when Helen stopped me to examine the tray.

"Who is that for?"

"Esther."

"No, it's not. Esther's on a low-sodium diet. She has coronary artery disease," she said sternly. "Always check the patient's charts."

I was embarrassed by the reprimand.

"I'm sorry. I know she has a pink tag. This afternoon she told me that she wanted me to bring her the ham dinner."

Helen nodded knowingly. "She sometimes cheats."

"How serious is her disease?"

"Serious as a heart attack."

"Is it curable?"

"It's treatable. They could try an arterial bypass if Esther allowed it, which she won't. I would never advocate it. At her age I don't think she would make it through the trauma of a medical procedure that heavy. So she takes medications to stabilize her condition." She patted my shoulder. "You've been doing a good job. Just be careful before giving the patients something to eat that's not on their chart. They always try to get away with things like this with the new guys."

"I won't let it happen again."

She started to walk away but abruptly stopped as if just remembering something. "You're working the late shift?"

I nodded.

"I didn't get a chance to walk Esther today and I've got to get home. Maybe this would be a good time for you to start. Take her around the third floor. About a half hour's worth." She added, "You might have to make her do it."

"Should I use a gait belt?"

"You should, but she won't let you. She says it makes her feel like a dog on a leash. Just lead her by the arm."

"Anything else?"

"Yes. Read the obituaries to her. The *Tribune*'s on my desk."

"The obituaries?"

"It is not a casual thing with Esther. Once I forgot to bring a paper in and I didn't hear the end of it until I had someone drive down to the *Tribune* office in Salt Lake and get her a back copy from that date."

I ran back downstairs to the cafeteria and

exchanged Esther's dinner, retrieved the newspaper from Helen's office, then climbed the stairway to Esther's room. From her partially open door came the mellifluous strains of an aged phonograph—a flowing, melodic symphony punctuated with sharp, staccato plucks from a dozen violins. I peered inside her room. Esther sat in her rocking chair with her eyes closed and her hand near her breast, caressing something that hung from the chain around her neck. It took me a moment to realize that her face was streaked with tears and she was softly crying, her chair moving slightly in time with the music. I knocked gently on the door and her eyes opened. She quickly wiped back her tears.

"Is that you, Helen?"

"It's me. Michael. I brought your dinner." I stepped into the room, setting the tray on a collapsible stand next to the bed. As I neared I could see that the pendant she had been fondling was the petite silver locket I had found the week before. I lifted the cover from her tray. "Dinner is served."

"That doesn't smell like ham."

"Helen stopped me on the way up. Apparently you tried to pull a fast one on me."

She did not answer the charge. "Where is Helen?" she demanded.

"She had errands to run, so she left early. She asked that I read you the obituaries, then take you out for exercise."

She made no attempt to conceal her disapproval. "You have the *Tribune*?"

"Right here."

"It must be the *Salt Lake City Tribune.* You can turn off the music."

I reached over to the boxy phonograph and lifted its needle from a well-worn vinyl record.

"Sit close enough that I can hear you. Your voice is soft."

"Don't you want to eat first?"

"No," she replied tersely.

I re-covered her dinner, then sat down on the bed next to her and ruffled open the paper to the obituaries and began to read. "Dennis Mecham, beloved husband and father, left this—"

"Not the whole thing. Just the names."

I glanced up. "Names it is." I proceeded along the page. When I had read the last of the announcements, I rolled the paper back up. "That's it."

"You read all of them?"

"Yes, ma'am."

"Are you certain?"

"There were only twelve today. You were expecting someone?"

"No one in particular." She crossed her hands in her lap and sat back quietly.

"I'll take you on your walk now, if you like."

"I don't need to walk."

"Gotta walk," I said as I stood. "You need exercise." I reached out to take her arm. She recoiled at my touch.

"I don't need to walk."

"Yes, you do."

Her face stiffened. "I will not walk with you."

Her stubbornness angered me. "If you want to veg out here on someone else's time, that's up to you. But I've got a job to do. And it will do you some good to get out of here."

"What do you know about my good? You're not a nurse. You don't have experience. You know nothing about caring for someone else."

It was neither the first nor the harshest of the indignities I had fielded from her, but there was something about what she said that cut deep, that flashed my temper, and I was as surprised by my reaction as she was.

"For the last two years I have done nothing *but* take care of someone else. I did everything for my mother, from spoon-feeding her to wiping up her vomit, right up until the minute she died. I think I know something about caring for someone."

My voice rang off in silence and Esther neither spoke nor moved but faced quietly ahead. I sighed in exasperation, embarrassed at my outburst. I conceded her the victory and stood to go when, without explanation, Esther slowly raised herself, extending her arm out to me. It was my first glimpse inside the shell of which Helen had spoken. I gently took her by the elbow and we began to walk. Though I had not before seen her out of the chair, she was not infirm and moved rather agilely, relying on me only for guidance. After fifteen minutes of pacing the third floor in solitude, she said, "You loved your mother, didn't you?"

"She was my best friend."

"I don't remember my mother. She died a week after I was born. My father raised me."

I didn't reply and she was suddenly withdrawn. Nothing more was said until we returned to her room. She felt for her bed, then sat down. "I wish to take a nap. Please shut my door when you leave."

I retrieved Helen's newspaper from the bureau. "Would you like your dinner warmed?"

She shook her head. "It will be all right."

"Then I'll be back tomorrow."

She stopped me at the doorway. "Michael."

"Yes?"

"Do you suppose life gives us second chances?"

"What do you mean?"

"If we've made a mistake in our lives, do you think that God or fate gives us a second chance to make it right?"

I considered the question. "I don't know. But we'd probably just make the same mistake over again."

Her countenance fell and her sadness resonated through her voice. "Thank you for reading to me."

I was unhappy to have contributed to her sadness. "Maybe I'm wrong. I just don't think I've seen any second chances in my life."

"Perhaps you don't know how to recognize them."

As I drove home that night I was still wondering what she meant.

chapter eight

The Christmas
Social

"An old acquaintance of my father's came through Betheltown today. He was on his way back from California where he has amassed a small fortune. He boasted greatly at my father's expense. There are those who go about their lives sharpening their egos on the grindstone of others' failures."

Excerpt from Esther Huish's Diary

Faye returned from Baltimore excited about school and the challenge of a new life in a new city. She also returned with an apartment and a date to inhabit it. Her departure was scheduled for December 28, which left us little more than three weeks together. Impending distance, I found, also makes the heart grow fonder, and as the calendar waned, I numbered the days with growing anxiety.

My lunchtime discussion with Alice had helped put my relationship with Faye in perspective. It was not that I hadn't considered marrying Faye, as she had requested of me;

more accurately, the opposite was true. I had considered it too deeply. And while it may be prudent to not leap until one looks, the longer one stands on the edge of a precipice, the less likely one is to jump, as one becomes more painfully aware of the length of the fall. It did not help me that there were so many shouting out the dangers.

The Murrows' annual Christmas party was a spectacular affair attended by most of Ogden's affluent, and the Murrow home was dressed as lavishly as the prosperous guests it anticipated receiving. Outside, the trees were awash in white-and-gold lights, and holly-and-pine garlands wound around the home's staircase bannister and light fixtures and anywhere else that lent itself to yule dressing. The home smelled of pine and wassail and perfumed candles. By dusk it was crowded with humanity.

Faye and I were sitting in the dining room surrounded by a dozen or so guests when Dr. Murrow entered the room accompanied by a broad-shouldered, gray-haired man and a woman who looked twenty years younger. His hand was behind the man while the other held a chardonnay. The man and woman also held drinks.

"There's my Faye," he proclaimed, gesturing toward her with the drink. "Faye, you remember Dr. and Mrs. Baird."

Mrs. Baird gawked. "I can't believe how you've blossomed. . . . You are just lovely."

Faye rose. "Thank you," she replied modestly.

"I understand that you are following in your father's footsteps," Mrs. Baird said.

"I am trying. Thanks in part to Dr. Baird. Thank you again, Doctor, for your letter of commendation."

The man smiled. "I'm glad that someone still considers it of merit. I understand it was of some efficacy."

"Yes. I was accepted to Johns Hopkins. It's a dream come true."

He raised his glass to her. "Congratulations. The letter was certainly penned without reservation. You will be an asset to the profession."

"Who is this handsome young man?" Mrs. Baird asked, looking toward me.

"This is Michael, my boyfriend," Faye said.

"So, Murrow, you'll be losing your daughter twice," the doctor said jovially.

Dr. Murrow did not find the observation amusing and his skin tightened over his cheeks. He looked down at me, then suddenly smiled maliciously. His voice boomed. "Ginny asked me to talk to these kids about how foolish it would be to get married so young, so I asked Michael how he plans to pay the rent. 'God will provide,' he said. So I asked him how he plans to put food on the table. 'God will provide,' he said again. I went back and told Ginny that the bad news is that our daughter is going to be homeless and hungry. The good news is that her boyfriend thinks I'm God."

The dining room crowd roared. Faye glared at her father indignantly. He noticed her wrath and turned to his guests. "Let me get you some more wine. Faye, give me a hand."

Faye set down her drink and left the room with him.

"Faye's always been one of our favorites," Mrs. Baird confided. "She is such a dear."

A few minutes later Faye returned alone. Her jaw was tight and her eyes were red rimmed. "Come on, Michael. We're leaving."

I set aside my punch. "What's wrong?"

"Just take me away from here."

As soon as we got to her car, she broke down crying.

"What happened back there?"

"You mean, besides being humiliated in front of everyone?"

"That's standard fare for your father."

"They are so mean. They are just so damn mean."

"What else happened, Faye?"

"For the first time, my mother got involved. She says that I'm tearing apart our family." She wiped back her eyes. "I love them, Michael. I don't want to hurt them." She looked up at me through swollen eyes. "What is so wrong with loving you?"

It hurt me to see Faye's pain, and while her father was the vehicle of that misery, I was the catalyst in its creation. In a sense, her father and I were both competing for the same woman, and such competitions, in nature or elsewhere, are never amiable. Unfortunately, I was the more easily removed from the equation. I had nothing to say of comfort, so I just quietly held her and ached with her for the pain that I brought.

chapter nine

The Doctor's
Threat

"Today, a Mr. Foster booked a room in the inn. He is a wealthy man and had come to Betheltown at the prospect of purchasing the Pate Mine. He spoke condescendingly to me as I served him his dinner. Then I suppose he decided me attractive as he expressed his desire for me to dine with him. I declined his offer. Rich company, like rich food, is often a cause of indigestion."

Excerpt from Esther Huish's Diary

I will never cease to be amazed by our species' keen ability for denial. Prior to my coming to the Arcadia, I had never given much thought to growing old or to those who had. It was not a conscious evasion, simply the consequence of circumstance. I didn't know anyone elderly. Both of my parents had died by the age of forty-five. I had no close grandparents, on my father's side by choice and on my mother's side by death, so the elderly remained to me people of a foreign culture, as removed from my everyday thoughts as the French—a culture I had occasional contact with, knew a few words of their native tongue, but had little relevance to my daily life. While this may be understandable, the difference to me is that we will not all be Parisians someday—but unless death plays its trump card in an early hand, we will all grow old. But like I said, we are keen at denial, and old age, like death, is always someone else's destination.

Wednesday morning, Helen wore a bright green sweater adorned with knit Christmas ornaments. She stopped to talk with me in the break room.

"I noticed on Esther's fitness schedule that you have her walking every day now."

"You seem surprised."

"Frankly, I am. No one beside me has ever been able to get her out of her room."

"You didn't think to tell me that?"

"I thought I'd just throw you into the lion's den and see if you came out alive."

I smirked. "It's probably better I didn't know that. She's a peculiar woman. Do you know much about her?"

"As much as anybody, I suppose. She came to us from a rest home in Bountiful. But she's originally from a small mining town called Bethel, out near Tooele. The place is just a ghost town now."

"How did you learn that?"

"I asked her." She handed me my schedule. "I see you're working for Alice on Christmas Eve."

"Is there a problem with that?"

"No. I just wanted to make sure she didn't coerce you into it."

"She didn't even ask."

"Just let me know if she becomes a problem," Helen said as she left the room.

Later that afternoon, for the first time, I took Esther walking on the second floor, reasoning that a change of scenery might be nice. It was for me, though, not her, as it didn't really matter to a blind woman. As we passed the closed door of room six I could hear Henri hacking inside.

I grimaced. "He sounds like he's getting worse. Do you know Henri?"

Esther nodded. "I'll tell you something about Henri."

I expected a great revelation about the silent man.

"Henri's old."

I grinned. "Everyone here is old."

"Henri's really old—even to me. He lost his leg in World War One. A shell took it off at the knee."

"How do you know that?"

"He told me."

"Henri speaks?"

"If he has a mind to. He just doesn't have much to say to most folk. Especially white folk. He doesn't trust them."

"Well, he needs to trust someone. I'm having trouble getting him to take his medication, and he won't stop smoking."

"Perhaps he doesn't want to get better."

"You think he wants to die?"

"He is all alone. His friends are all dead. He is a decorated war hero, but is put in diapers. Would you want to keep living?"

"Probably not," I decided.

"No," she gently echoed. "Probably not."

As I contemplated her words, there was suddenly screaming down the hallway.

"Just a moment," I said. I left Esther standing next to the wall and ran around the corner to investigate the commotion. Near the second-floor landing a cluster of residents surrounded Della and Edna, who had squared off in their wheelchairs, metal to metal, their fists raised for combat. Before I could reach them they went at each other, and Edna grabbed Della's hair and yanked her back, while Della issued forth a shrill scream. I pried my way into the brawl, catching a hand across my cheek as I pushed the two wheelchairs apart. Sharon arrived just then and stood back to watch my handling of the conflict.

"Ladies, what's going on here?"

The women stared hatefully at each other. Edna was the first to speak, pointing a willowy finger in accusation.

"This common thief stole my purse." She turned to Della, her face further contorting in fury. "If I had a flatiron I'd show you what for."

I faced Della, who was still panting heavily. "Is it true, Della?"

"I found that purse. I didn't know it was hers."

"Della, give Edna her purse back."

Della did not respond but stared vehemently at her accuser.

"She can't give it back," Edna said impatiently. "She lost it."

Della looked suddenly penitent.

"Is that true, Della? You've already lost it?"

"Not 'already,'" Edna piped in. "Back in forty-two."

"Della took your purse forty years ago and you are just getting mad at her now?"

"I just remembered it," Edna said.

Sharon covered her mouth to keep from laughing out loud, then stepped forward and took the handles of Della's chair. "C'mon, Della. I'll take you downstairs."

With the women separated, I returned to Esther, who had groped her way along the wall to a chair. I sat down next to her.

"Sorry I stranded you here."

"That's all right. Della and Edna at it again over the purse?"

"They've done this before?"

"Every few weeks Edna remembers that purse and goes after Della."

I shook my head. "That poor woman."

"Della shouldn't even be in here."

"Why is that?"

"She had her own home bought and paid for. A place she could dig in her own garden. She liked to do that. Had her own flower garden."

"What happened to it?"

"Her children in Seattle invited her up for a visit, then sold the place out from under her. They claimed they did it for her own good, but they just wanted their inheritance. They decided Della was living too long, so they just took it. It is despicable," she said tersely.

"I believe there are special lakes in hell reserved for people who prey on the defenseless."

"Then you believe in hell," she said.

"It's easier to believe in than heaven."

"I believe in hell. And in heaven. But I think they're the same place."

"How is that?"

"I believe death wakens us to the consequences of our actions—to feel the sorrow or joy we have caused in our lifetime. The location is irrelevant."

"What of the talk of fire and brimstone?"

"It is figurative. How else could such torment be described?"

"It would be just," I decided.

"I believe heaven is just," Esther said. She suddenly asked, "Where are you from, Michael?"

"I was born in Cheyenne, but we moved a lot. I was only twelve when my mother and I came to Ogden."

"What part of Ogden?"

"Initially, wherever we parked. We lived in a twenty-year-old station wagon for about six months."

"Where was your father?"

"I don't know. By then it was pretty much moot." I looked around. "Ready to start walking again?"

Esther nodded and I stood, helping her up. Sharon approached.

"Michael, there's a gentleman waiting downstairs to see you. A distinguished-looking, impatient gentleman."

"I'm not expecting anyone."

"Perhaps he's from the university," she ventured. "I'll finish with Esther, if you like."

I squeezed Esther's hand. "We're not going to make it through this today."

"Go see your visitor," Esther said.

Sharon took Esther's arm and I made my way downstairs. On the main floor, Dr. Murrow sat on one of the burgundy vinyl chairs near the front counter. The last I had seen of him was a few nights back at the Murrows' Christmas party. He looked up, casually following my descent.

"Hello, Michael."

"Dr. Murrow. What brings you here?"

He pushed himself up from his knees and reached out his hand. I took it awkwardly.

"Sorry to interrupt your work. I thought I would come by and see if you would be so kind as to dine with me tonight." He spoke with uncharacteristic pleasantness, and it struck me as odd.

"I'm not off until six. But Faye's out tonight with some of her girlfriends."

"Faye needn't join us. I thought it would be just the two of us. I could pick you up around six."

If this was an ambush, I wanted my own means of retreat. "I'll meet you."

"La Fleur de Lis around six? My treat, of course," and he smiled again. We both knew it was an offer I couldn't refuse.

"Six it is."

"Splendid. I'll be waiting."

I wondered what he was waiting for.

A quarter after six I arrived at the luxurious French restaurant. The parking lot was a showcase of the automotive elite: bright sports cars with feminine curves and liquid shines and the hubris-polished, chrome-grilled cars of European descent. The valet gazed at my car in amusement.

"Want me to park it for you?"

"Yeah. Why not?"

I handed him my keys and entered the dimly lit restaurant. The maître d' followed my entrance with disapproval, then, without comment, disappeared into the cloakroom and brought me out a navy jacket.

"Perhaps you'd feel more comfortable in this," he said haughtily. Just then Dr. Murrow emerged from the sconce-lit dining room. He was dressed impeccably in a dark wool suit, single breasted, with a red silk tie adorned with a coat-of-arms pattern. On his lapel was a gold AMA pin.

"Michael. I'm glad you could make it," he said as if he had doubted my arrival. "I've reserved us a place."

I followed him back to an oblong table set for two with crystal goblets before sculpted cloth napkins and a linen-lined basket of baguette and an opened bottle of scotch. In the center of the table, a small silver vase held fresh hyacinths. He motioned to my seat, then sat down himself. He immediately reached for the bottle. "Have you ever had the pleasure of drinking Laphroaig?"

"No, sir."

"It's a magnificent scotch. Wonderful flavor, dry, peat and heather overtones."

I thought he sounded like an advertisement. "Actually, I don't drink."

"This may cure you of that," he said, pouring me a glass. "I'm prescribing a dram—a little libation is good for the heart."

"My father used to say that."

The doctor was not pleased with the comparison. "So, you are a teetotaler."

"Yes, sir."

"Call me Ben." He poured himself a glass of the scotch and sipped it slowly, which I thought he did more for me than himself.

"It defies even scientists why scotch cannot be made anywhere but in Scotland. Business deals are always sealed with a dram. It is the drink of farewell and completion."

I wondered why he was telling me this. A tuxedo-ensembled waiter appeared, flicked open our napkins, laid them across our laps, then presented open menus, the entrées described in scripted French. I could have fed myself for a week on the cost of an entrée.

"Have you dined here before?" the doctor asked.

I looked up from my menu. "No. It's not exactly in my budget."

He nodded smugly and I knew that I had delivered another arrow to his quiver. Honesty was always one of my weaknesses.

"I recommend the chateaubriand. If you like shellfish, the *les coquilles* is also quite good. It is served in a cognac sauce." He looked at me condescendingly. "I think that should be all right for a teetotaler."

I ignored his remark as I looked back down at the menu. A moment later Dr. Murrow raised his hand and a waiter advanced to our table.

"What may I bring you tonight, Dr. Murrow?"

"The chateaubriand and the field-greens salad with your house vinaigrette."

"And you, sir?"

"I'll have the same," I said.

The waiter took our menus.

Dr. Murrow tore a piece of bread. "I once considered that I might be a chef. I enjoy cooking. Rarely get the chance to get to it, though. Of course, Ginny's no slouch in the kitchen."

"Is Mrs. Murrow out tonight?"

"No," he succinctly replied.

As the evening advanced, the doctor

spoke with increasing casualness, as if we were frequent dinner companions or drinking buddies, and this had the effect of causing me greater trepidation. It was not until our entrées were delivered that he offered the first clue about his agenda. He lifted his glass. "I am certain that you are speculating as to why I wish to speak with you. We have not been exactly"—he cautiously chose the word—"friendly."

I awaited his explanation.

"Frankly, I wanted to apologize for how I have treated you. There is more to you than I've given you credit for."

"More?"

"I have concluded that you're not just some love-struck kid out looking for a pretty skirt. I believe that you really do love my daughter."

I was astonished at his admission. "I care deeply about Faye."

"My point," he said quickly. "I believe that you do. And what is love if it's not that?" He cut into his tenderloin, speared it, then smiled as he chewed. "Love is such a trite expression these days—we men like the way a woman looks and we claim a state of love like we might an ailment. But there is more to love than that, isn't there?"

"I've always believed so."

"It took me years to understand that when you truly care about someone, you must focus on more than your own desires. To truly love something is not to desire a thing, but to desire its happiness. That's why love requires sacrifices. Sometimes painful ones." He paused for emphasis. "Some of the other boys Faye brings home I could never have this conversation with, but you're different. You understand my meaning."

His casual injection of "other boys" stung me, but I did not show it. "I think that I do."

"I don't need to tell you that life is hard. You never know what's around the next bend, and sometimes it knocks the wind out of you. That's the way marriage is as well. How often do you see a couple years down the line still staring goo-goo eyed at each other? It just doesn't happen." He leaned forward, his brow bent in grave inquiry. "Do you know why?"

"No, sir."

"It is because romantic love is an illusion. It portends an eternal round of ecstatic bliss with love conquering all. That's how all relationships start. But then the silver lining begins to tarnish and the honeymoon ends. Pretty soon she's complaining because you haven't been out to dinner for a month and there's not enough in the bank account, even while your boss is breaking your back." He took another drink. "All relationships start on fire. But the embers cool."

"Is that how it is with you and Mrs. Murrow?"

He didn't like my question, and for the first time I detected the anger that simmered beneath his calm facade. Then, inexplicably, his lips rose in a whimsical smile as if we had been playfully sparring and I had just scored a point.

"You do understand that romance will disappear. And then what have you? Only the life that you have built for yourselves."

I shifted uncomfortably in my chair. "It may sound naive, but I think you're wrong. I believe it's after the honeymoon ends that true love begins. It's in the hard times that the greater virtues of love reveal themselves, like tolerance and patience and kindness."

He cut me off. "Of course, that's the ideal. But where is the ideal? It's always a marriage away, isn't it? For instance, do you think that your mother loved your father when she met him?"

The reference to my parents caught me off guard.

"Of course she did."

"And he loved her?"

"I suppose so."

His mouth curled in a cruel, knowing grin. "And how did that all end up?"

I set my napkin on the table. "My father was an alcoholic."

"We all have weaknesses, don't we? Only a fool claims to not. So, where did that leave your mother? Did his love save her?"

"It left my mother in a world of hurt."

"You're a smart boy, Michael. You might make someone very happy, if you can hold it all together. But how far does the apple fall from the tree?"

"As far as it needs to."

"Maybe. In the rare case. But no one really knows. So, are you going to experiment with my Faye? Is that love?" His eyes were fierce. "It's ironic, isn't it? If you love Faye, you must let her go. If you care only about yourself, then you'll pursue her. It's not an easy decision, but it's a clear one."

I said nothing, biting back my growing anger.

"Mind you, I do not say this to demean my daughter, but you must take it to heart. Faye is a free spirit. A compassionate, free spirit.

Always the one to bring home the lost puppy. But there comes a price with that kind of spontaneity. Has Faye ever told you about her first car?"

I folded my arms awaiting the story.

". . . A black-and-gold Pontiac Trans Am with a T-roof. For an entire year it was all she talked about. As far as Faye was concerned there was no other car. Being the dutiful parent, on her sixteenth birthday, along with her driver's license, I saw to it that she got that car. It was less than three months before she wanted something else. The next model." He paused for the analogy to settle. "Faye's off to a new world, with a lot of handsome, clever boys from good homes and good lives. You don't really think that you can compete with that, do you? She may be content with a Trans Am now, but what happens when she rides in a Ferrari?" He took another drink as he ascertained how this was affecting me. "I would just hate to see you tossed aside for the next model. Faye leaves next Thursday. Maybe it's time to take your exit."

I pushed back from the table. "It is time to take my exit."

He realized my intent and waved as if it had all been in play. "No, no, sit down, enjoy your meal. You've hardly touched it."

"I guess I'm not used to rich foods."

His countenance abruptly changed and his eyes narrowed in loathing. "I want to be very clear about something. I didn't raise Faye for twenty-something years to throw it away on you. Faye's a smart girl; I believe she will move on of her own accord. But she is a volatile personality and it wouldn't be the first time she has made a rash decision or a poor choice. So let me make things a little clearer for you. If Faye ends up engaged or committed to you in any permanent way, I will cut her off. No MasterCard. No tuition. No Johns Hopkins. No playing doctor."

"You would never take that away from her."

He did not wince. "Faye has two younger sisters that I must consider." He leaned back confidently, his scotch in hand. "Frankly, all I would be doing is giving her a premature taste of what life with you would be like. Am I wrong?"

"You're a liar."

His gaze was as black and hard as onyx. "Think of it as tough love."

chapter ten

The Dilemma

"The most difficult of decisions are often not the ones in which we cannot determine the correct course, rather the ones in which we are certain of the path but fear the journey."

Excerpt from Esther Huish's Diary

There was little new about the doctor's invective—he had only given voice to the specter that had shadowed me since I first met Faye. In the faithless corners of my mind I had always expected her to move on. But if our relationship was an issue of faith, Faye had never given me reason to doubt. I could not say the same of myself. In truth, I didn't know just how much of my father's weaknesses I had inherited. I loathed my father for this. Not just for who he was, but for who I was because of him. There was something about my father's ghost that I could not exorcise, and numbered among my greatest fears was to someday look into a mirror only to see him staring back.

Still, these fears could be relegated to the future. The doctor's threat to withhold funding from Faye's schooling, however, added immediate weight to our dilemma. His timing was impeccable, connivingly so, and if he had played that threat, counting on the possibility of my love to be a deterrent to our relationship, he had gambled correctly—I did love Faye more than myself. To threaten Faye's dreams at the verge of inception was something I could not do, no matter how he had manipulated the circumstance—even if he himself was the source of that pain.

It is, perhaps, the greatest irony of love. That which we truly love, we must be willing to give up for its own benefit. And in this I knew how much Faye meant to me. For as breathless as the possibility of losing her left me, there was no question in my mind that I would lay down my heart as a stepping-stone for her to reach her dreams. To do less would be a counterfeit of love, a forgery with no value other than what self-indulgent fraud could be had of it. That's what I knew. At least, that's what I thought I knew. What I had not factored into the equation, perhaps never dared to, is that I was the greater part of her dreams.

My decision to not tell Faye about the dinner conversation required no great effort of deliberation. Faye had suffered enough pain for our relationship, and I had no desire to contribute to its accumulation. I probably would have never shared it with anyone if Esther hadn't asked. With me at her arm, she had just completed the first pass of her floor when we sat down to rest near the nurses' station. "Was your visitor from the university?"

I frowned. "Unfortunately not. It was Faye's father."

"What did he want?"

"Same thing he always wants—me out of his daughter's life."

"Why is that?"

"He considers me white trash. He expects Faye to marry someone from a wealthy family with social prominence. He is certain that all I can promise his daughter is to keep her barefoot and pregnant."

"He doesn't think you will someday be successful?"

"I don't think we share the same idea of success."

"What does Faye think of this?"

"It's really hard on her. Her father forces the issue so that Faye must choose between him and me. Last night he threatened to cut Faye off financially if she ends up in any permanent relationship with me."

"Would he?"

"I think he would. The man's evil." I sighed. "I feel like I've been checkmated. I don't know what's worse—an absentee father like mine was, or a ubiquitous one like hers."

"That is the first time you have mentioned your father to me."

"He was no father," I said contemptuously. I raked my hand back through my hair. "Faye's expecting a commitment. If I give her one, if she takes it, she loses her dreams. If I don't, I could lose her."

"What will you do?"

"I don't know." I looked down the hallway and for a moment watched Grace as she pushed her walker down the hall.

"How about your love, Esther? What about Thomas?"

I could not have predicted the effect of that name or the dramatic change in mood it would evoke.

"Where did you see that name?" she asked fiercely. Before I could answer she said, "You read my letters."

"What letters?"

Her face flushed. "You had no right to read my letters. You had no right to get into my drawer."

I glanced about, as several of the residents were now watching. "I didn't read your letters, Esther. I don't know what letters you mean. That name was inscribed on the back of your locket. The one I found that day . . ."

She covered her face with her hands. "I would like you to take me back to my room."

I waited for her emotion to settle, then I slowly rose, taking her by the arm. She said nothing as I escorted her back.

"I'm really sorry," I said contritely. "I didn't mean to upset you." I helped her to her chair. "It was just written on the locket."

Her hand caressed the oblong pendant and she still didn't speak, and so I left the room, thinking about Thomas and her mysterious letters and what they might have to do with each other.

I returned home that night to a letter of my

own—correspondence printed on University of Utah letterhead. A letter of congratulations to the newest recipient of the university's presidential scholarship.

chapter eleven

Christmas Eve

"It was a festive Christmas Eve in Betheltown, and we gathered at the church to sing and worship and feast. I returned near midnight and shortly afterward a couple came to the inn seeking lodging. We had no vacancy and as I was about to turn them out, the great irony of the circumstance was manifest. I gave them my room for the night and slept in the kitchen."

Excerpt from Esther Huish's Diary

December 24 fell with heavy snow that clung tenaciously to the roads until the highway patrol issued a travelers' advisory and began stopping cars at the base of the canyon to inspect for snow tires or tire chains. And still it fell, sealing in the solemnity of the day.

Let it snow, I thought. Christmas had already come, packaged in the bright wrappings of a full-ride scholarship to the University of Utah. But if I was euphoric, I seemed staid in comparison to Faye. She had received the news with such elation that an outside observer would have thought that she had won the award. She insisted on braving the snowy canyons to bring me dinner and a bottle of nonalcoholic wine to celebrate my achievement. She stayed for more than an hour, until I made her go, concerned by the worsening road conditions. I held her arm as I walked her out to her car, and watched her cautiously descend the canyon until her car's taillights were no longer visible.

From the roadway the Arcadia appeared dark, an eclipse that carried inside to its sullen corridors, obscuring the plastic chains and decorations that I would soon bring down. I returned inside to help with the residents' dinner. For the holiday's forgotten ones, the cafeteria served instant potatoes and pressed turkey with canned cranberry sauce and a bread pudding of questionable consistency. A local church's plans to sing carols was canceled when the weather turned inclement, so most of the residents simply went to bed as if it were any other night, though a few gathered around the dayroom television to watch *It's a Wonderful Life,* hoping to provoke some semblance of the season's spirit. By the end of my shift the home was still, disrupted only by the distant and frequent echo of Henri's strained hack.

It was my first Christmas Eve without my mother, and the sadness of that thought had eaten away at the day's euphoria. I was saddened that my mother was not here to hear the news of my scholarship. She would have been proud, as she should be, for it would have been more her honor than mine. Then I remembered that I had not yet told Esther about the award. I was still embarrassed by my previous night's faux pas with regard to Esther, and I suspect that I had subconsciously avoided her even though I had brought her a Christmas present—a peace offering of fruitcake—which I thought to bestow upon her at the first convenient opportunity. That opportunity had never come, and I assumed that by this hour my chance was past, as she had likely been whisked away for Christmas Eve festivities in the home of some nearby relative. I clocked out and had already donned my coat and gloves when I decided to just leave the gift in her room.

I climbed the stairway and knocked softly at her door, then, expecting to find the room vacant, slowly opened it. The room was dark except for the weak illumination of a single low-wattage lamp on her nightstand. To my surprise, Esther sat alone in the darkness, her eyelids fluttering with the weight of fatigue. I stepped into the room.

"Esther?"

She spoke without turning. "Hello, Michael."

I laid my gloves on her bureau, then sat down on the bed next to her.

"I brought you something." I set the ornate, paisley-adorned tin in her lap. "It's a fruitcake."

She clasped both hands over the gift, running her slender fingers across the container's tin lip. "That was very thoughtful of you." She looked very sad. "It snowed today, didn't it?"

I looked toward the undraped window, the navy sky dotted by white flakes. "It's still snowing. The roads are pretty bad."

"You didn't have an automobile accident, did you?"

"No. I got here all right."

"I don't care much for snow. You can slip on it and break a hip."

"I imagine so."

"... doctors like snow, I think. It keeps them in country clubs, fixing all those broken hips."

"I've never really thought of it like that." The room fell quiet. I threaded my fingers together in my lap. "Do you have plans for tonight?"

She nodded, her gesture betrayed by a forlorn countenance. "My son is coming for me."

"Good," I said.

"Have you plans?"

"No. Just work. I'm off now, though."

"Why aren't you with that girl of yours?"

"Faye's spending the night with her family. We were planning to spend tomorrow together."

"I expect that will be lovely."

The melancholy was suffocating. "Well, I best be on my way. Before the roads get much worse."

"Thank you," she said. I took my gloves from the bureau and shoved them into my pockets. "I wanted to apologize again. About the other day. It wasn't any of my business."

Again, Esther did not respond to my apology.

"Well, Merry Christmas."

"And to you, Michael," she said softly.

I quickly stepped from the room, closed the door behind me, and descended the stairs. Sharon had just arrived at the front counter for the night shift, and my approach startled her.

"Hi, Michael. I thought Alice was scheduled for tonight."

"She wanted it off and I needed the money."

"I hear you. Christmas always leaves me broke. That's why I'm working. It was either work or wassail and caroling at Aunt Maud's."

I glanced down at my watch. "Do you know what time Esther's son is coming for her?"

She looked at me quizzically. "Esther doesn't have any children."

"Are you certain?"

"Esther hasn't had a visitor in the three years I've been here. She had a surgery a few years back and when I checked her file for next of kin, the line was blank. Makes you wonder where people like her come from. It's Eleanor Rigbyish."

I looked back toward the stairway for a moment, then turned to leave.

"I'll see you Monday."

"Have a good Christmas."

Outside, the snow fell steadily, gathering in vertical blankets across the craggy walls of the canyon, reflecting the moon's light in a translucent glow. The road was silent, abandoned of travelers, who had settled in for the night's festivities or maybe just sleep. I suspect that it was my own loneliness that turned me around. Sharon looked up as I walked back in.

"Forget something?"

"I left something upstairs."

I climbed the stairs to Esther's room and knocked gently.

"Esther?" I pushed open her door. Esther was still in her chair, her eyes closed, her hands still clasped over the tin.

"Did you forget something, Michael?"

"I forgot to tell you I won the scholarship."

Despite her sadness she smiled. "I am so pleased. You must be very excited."

"It's the first thing I've ever won." I was glad that she was pleased. I walked to her side, then sat down on the bed next to her. "What time is your son coming by?"

"About eight."

"It's nearly nine-thirty."

"He must be detained. You said the roads aren't very good."

Her lie filled me with sadness. "Esther." I paused, uncertain if I was right to speak, but somehow unable to constrain myself. "Esther. You don't have a son."

Esther said nothing, and while I wondered what idiocy had possessed me, a single tear streamed down her cheek and she brushed it back. Then her voice fell wearily. "I did once, Michael."

Tears began to fall copiously and she no longer made an effort to wipe them back. I took a tissue from her nightstand and placed it in her hand and she dabbed her eyes. I put my hand on hers.

"Tell me about him."

"His name was Matthew. He was my sweet boy."

I asked softly, "Where is Matthew?"

"He's gone." She lowered her head into her hands. "Matthew was severely retarded. In forty-eight I came down with the scarlet fever, and because I was alone, the state took Matthew to an institution. It would only be for a time. How could he know that he would be coming back?" Her eyes again filled with tears. "He stopped living without me. How could he have known?"

"I'm sorry." I looked at the photograph of the soldier as I thought a piece to the puzzle had been given to me. "The picture on your bureau—the soldier is Matthew's father?"

She shook her head and her tone changed from grief to insolence. "No. I have no photographs of Matthew's father. I don't want any. He was no father."

"I understand. I don't want any photographs of my father either."

She continued to dab her eyes.

"Who is the soldier?"

Esther did not speak for more than a minute. It was as if she stood before some great, sealed book, contemplating whether or not to breach its cover. Suddenly she said dolefully, "The soldier is Thomas. He is the only man I have ever loved . . . perhaps the only to truly love me."

I was astonished that she had shared such a thing.

"But you never married him."

Her countenance suddenly took on a far-away demeanor. "I was married before him and after him. But never to him."

"Why?"

She did not answer, but blinked slowly as if it were a question she had not considered. She suddenly asked, "Did Faye get a fruitcake too?"

I could not help but smile. "No. We haven't exchanged gifts yet, but I plan to give her a book and a locket. I got the idea when I found your locket."

She nodded and I suspect that she was pleased to have inspired the gift.

"I've never seen a locket like yours, Esther. I couldn't tell if it's gold or silver."

"It was originally gold. It was silver-plated."

"Why would someone silver-plate gold?"

"It was illegal to export gold from some countries. So immigrants would silver-plate their jewelry so that they could take it with them. Thomas's mother was from Romania. It was once hers." She touched the pendant. "A locket keeps dear things near."

"That's what I thought. Faye's going away to school in a few days."

"What book did you purchase for her?"

"Milton's *Paradise Lost*. It was one of my mother's favorites."

"It is a beautiful book," Esther said. Then,

speaking gently, as if savoring the words, she recited:

Of Man's first disobedience, and the fruit
Of that forbidden tree whose mortal taste
Brought death into the world, and all our
     woe,
With loss of Eden, till one greater Man
Restore us and regain the blissful seat . . .

"You know the work."

Esther smiled, flattered that I approved of her recitation. "I don't suppose anyone really knows the work. Just a few verses. I believe some things aren't from this world. It is as if God borrows some souls to share such great gifts."

"My mother said that once. She didn't have much to give materially, so she gave me literature. She read to me every night up until I was a teenager. Not just children's books, but classics like Hawthorne and Dickens. When she was bedridden—before she died—I read to her."

"Then you were rich."

"That's the first time I've been accused of that." I thought reminiscently of my mother. "I suppose I was."

"Do you write, Michael?"

"I've tried my hand at poetry."

"I would like to hear some of your work."

"It isn't good."

"I am certain that it is better than the fruit-cake you brought me."

I looked at her in astonishment, then we both burst out in spontaneous laughter. It was the first time I had heard her laughter.

". . . I'm sorry, that was not polite."

"I'm not offended. I don't know anyone who likes fruitcake. I figured that it must be your generation."

"It was foisted upon my generation too."

"I've heard it said there is really only one fruitcake and it is passed around the world each year."

She laughed again and her countenance seemed lighter as her voice trailed off in a pleased sigh. "I would like to hear your poetry."

"I've never shared it."

"Then you don't share yourself."

I considered her words. "All right. This is something I wrote for Faye." I breathed in deeply.

To harrowed darkness came such light,
From lofty realms of hope descends,

To where the quiet, broken lay,
Despairing, sullen realm of night.

Amidst the dark, a brilliant sun,
She lifts the shards of shattered dreams,
And pressed the sharp against her heart,
With her sweet blood she made them one.

After a moment Esther asked gently, "What was Faye's response?"

"Faye has never heard it."

Esther seemed more saddened than surprised. "No, you don't share yourself," she repeated.

"Maybe I don't," I countered. "But you never told me why you didn't marry the soldier."

Esther lowered her head and then, with shame in her voice, said despondently, "Sometimes we fear the good more than the bad." She closed her eyes and lay back in her chair, and within a few moments her breathing grew heavier and I didn't know if she was asleep or wanted me to believe that she was. I watched her for a moment, then said, "Merry Christmas, Esther." I stooped over and kissed her on the cheek. "To you and your soldier." I left her to her dreams.

chapter twelve

Paradise Lost

"There comes to each life at least one Betheltown. But it comes only once and we dare not ask for more."

Excerpt from Esther Huish's Diary

At least Christmas started out well. The first sheaths of dawn illuminated the valley, and the blue winter sky cut crisply against a gleaming horizon of crystalline snow. Faye arrived around ten wearing the new ski parka that her parents had given her that morning and an umber wool headband. Her cheeks were rosy and her breath clouded before her. She rang the doorbell with her elbow as her arms were full of presents, three brightly wrapped boxes.

"Make way for Santa's helper," she said, smiling gleefully.

"You're an imposter," I said. "Mrs. Claus would never allow you near the old man."

Her smile spread. "Merry Christmas, handsome."

She brought the presents into the kitchen and laid them on the table, then walked back out. She returned carrying a long garment bag. She unzipped it to reveal a navy pea jacket. The kind the rich collegiates were all wearing.

"You'll need this for school," she said.

"You spoil me."

"That's my goal."

I went to my room and retrieved my gifts for her. I noticed that she examined the smaller of the boxes with great interest.

"Do you want to open gifts now?" I asked.

"Let's wait until we get back. Anticipation is the better part of most pleasures." She glanced down at her watch. "I didn't realize it was so late. We better go. They'll be expecting us."

Faye had promised a grand surprise for the morning. "Who'll be expecting us?"

She beamed. "That's my surprise."

We went out to her car and I found the backseat filled with presents. "Who is all this for?"

"We're taking Christmas to a family," Faye said excitedly. "Our sorority has been working all month on a Sub-for-Santa, and I was elected to chair the committee."

Our destination was a neighborhood only a few blocks from my home, closer to the viaducts. The house was not much different from mine, in size or architecture, though it showed the influence of children; the aluminum siding and front door were scribbled with crayons, and children's snow toys littered the yard. I suspect my neighborhood had more than its share of such charitable visits. Faye pulled into the driveway, then walked up to the door and knocked. A gaunt Mexican woman opened, spoke, glanced out to the car, then opened the torn screen door, latching it back for us to enter. Faye gestured for me to come, so I began the chore of gathering the presents and carrying them inside, where there was a small plastic tree in the corner of the room with a few baubles hanging from it, walnuts painted with glue and pressed in green and gold glitter with yarn loops for hanging and a few paper snowflakes. There was another woman in the room who held a child to her breast that I guessed to be four or five years of age.

It took four trips to bring in all the presents, and as I stacked them in the corner, the room filled with spectators, a half dozen children with dirty faces and black hair. They watched in quiet wonderment.

It should have been a joyful experience. For most people, I think, it would have been so. The kind of event to record in the Christmas photo album of their minds and walk away thanking providence for their own blessings. Instead, I sat there looking at the children's blank stares and I saw myself looking back from a black looking glass of memory. It was another reminder of the disparity between Faye and me.

I remember the one year the Sub-for-Santa came to our house. I was five years old and I stood behind my mother holding tightly to her skirt when the strangers entered our tiny apartment. They were from the local Church of the Nazarene and they came graciously bearing food and presents, led by a woman who looked like Doris Day and smelled like the perfume section of the downtown department stores. She was loud and filled with the holiday spirit. My mother did all she could to express her gratitude, though she was clearly embarrassed to be the recipient of the charity. Had it not been for me, such charity would nowise have been a consideration. As usual, she put aside her battered pride and bore the humiliation with dignity and thankfulness.

As she placed the ham they had brought into the refrigerator, there was a sudden clatter at the door and my old man stumbled in stinking drunk. He was unshaven and disheveled and smelled more like he had bathed in liquor than drunk it. The group stared at him as he swaggered past them, eyeing them all maliciously.

"Who the hell are you?" he shouted, his voice slurred with inebriation. My mother stepped in front of our guests, her face blushed in humiliation. Her voice wavered. "They are from the church. You just leave them be. They have brought Christmas presents for Michael."

My drunken father blasphemed, then yelled at the church people, "Get the hell out of my house. All of you. Get the hell out."

The Doris Day woman looked at my mother sympathetically, then one of the men with a soprano voice but the hulking body of a barroom bouncer walked up next to my mother.

"Do you want me to take care of him?" He asked dutifully, his lip curled in indignation. My father gazed up at the large man fearfully. My mother was now crying and shook her head.

"You're sure now, ma'am? He's not going to lay a finger on you?"

"No. He doesn't beat me," she said matter-of-factly.

He touched my mother's arm as he coolly stared down my father, then he stepped back in with the group, who were now flocked near the doorway. I suspect that they usually left with a carol, but they wouldn't today.

"Merry Christmas, Mrs. Keddington. And to you, son," the Doris Day woman said, echoed by our other benefactors.

"Thank you. God bless you all," my mother said. Biting down on her lip, she took my hand and led me to the bedroom to open my gifts. The next year my mother took on extra work at Christmastime.

As I gazed at the huddled children I felt sullen and distant, like a wall had crashed down between Faye and me, and Faye looked at me quizzically. She did not understand—likely could not understand. She was filled with the resultant joy of charity and did not comprehend why I had inversely become suddenly morose.

To bond with another is to marry a lifetime of accumulated experiences, and this episode reminded me of how little Faye really knew of me. I was quiet for the rest of the morning, and we went to Faye's aunts for a late Christmas luncheon, then returned to my place shortly before dusk. Though Faye tried to appear cheerful, my moodiness was clearly disturbing to her.

"Let's exchange gifts," Faye said brightly as we entered the house. She brought her packages into the living room. "Open this one first." She handed me a small, brightly wrapped gift, which I quickly opened. Inside was a Sony Walkman cassette player with headphones. The next unveiling revealed music for the player—a four-cassette Beatles anthology. The last package was a picture frame, which I gladly assumed was a picture of Faye.

To my surprise I unveiled a beautiful black-and-white photograph of my mother in her bridal gown. I did not remember ever seeing this picture of her, and there was something haunting about it. It took a minute to realize what it was about the portrait that I found so curious. My mother appeared confident. There was a pluck to her demeanor that I had never seen before. I was mesmerized by it. "Where did you get this?" I asked.

"I had it enlarged from a picture I found in your attic. I have a key, remember?" I didn't respond and she asked, "Do you like it?"

Her query broke my spell. "It's really beautiful. Thank you." I laid it against the wall. "Now open yours."

She chose to first open the larger of the two gifts.

"It's a book," she exclaimed as she pulled back the paper. "*Paradise Lost*. Is there significance to this?"

"It's just one of my favorites."

She thumbed through a few of its pages, then set it aside and lifted the smaller box. As obvious as it would be to every woman on the planet, it was only as she lifted the small jewelry box that it occurred to me that she was expecting something else. She slowly unwrapped it, then opening the velvet box, gazed in dismay at the locket. After a moment she smiled, though I sensed that she was biting back her disappointment. "It's beautiful." She pried it open.

"There's not a picture of you in it."

"I didn't want to be presumptuous."

"Most men are good at presumptuous." She again forced a smile. "Find me a picture. I want to fix this now."

I fetched a pair of scissors and a box of snapshots from the other room, and Faye selected one with the right proportions, then trimmed it down until it fit snugly inside the casing. The locket's chain was long and instead of opening its clasp, she lifted the piece over her head. It fell over her blouse against her breast. "Now I can carry you near my heart as well as in it." It was characteristic of Faye to put a positive spin on things when she really wanted to cry.

"You don't like it," I said.

She frowned. "No. That's not it at all."

"You thought it was going to be something else."

"No," she lied. "It's fine. Everything is just fine," she said unconvincingly. She did not cry but touched the corner of her eye. Suddenly, she conceded, "All right, I did. I've been practically giddy all day because I actually thought you were going to ask me to marry you tonight. I've been waiting all day like some kind of an idiot."

"Faye, don't do this."

"I just thought . . ." She turned back and her eyes were wet. ". . . why didn't you, Michael?"

The question hung dangerously between our hearts.

"It's just the way things are between us," I replied solemnly.

"Between us? What kind of things?" She looked at me incredulously. "What is wrong with 'us'?"

I did not answer, and her countenance fell as if she had just understood the extent of my distancing.

"Michael, I'm not going to see you again for sixteen weeks. You can't leave me like this. You owe me an explanation."

"I don't know what to say."

Her voice grew more ardent. "Three weeks ago we're talking about marriage, and today you don't know what to say?" She glanced down at the locket and her voice fell, then she again looked at me sharply. "I just want to know one thing. Do you have any intention of asking me to marry you?"

I turned away from her piercing gaze. "I don't know."

Faye's eyes welled with tears. "I can't believe this is happening. You don't know? What part don't you know? If you love me? If I'm the one you want to spend the rest of your life with?" A tear streamed down her cheek and her voice cracked. "Help me understand what part it is that you don't know."

My chest ached. "Faye, I can't give you the life you're used to."

"No," she shouted angrily. "Don't get noble with me. This isn't about me or the quality of my life. I know what I want. This is about you and your damn insecurities."

The accusation ignited me. "What do you know about insecurity? When was the last time someone delivered Christmas to your doorstep? When was the last time your mother went hungry so you could eat? You don't even know what a food stamp looks like."

Faye gazed at me incredulously, then her expression abruptly changed and a look of enlightenment crossed her face. "You talked to my father."

I didn't reply, confirming her accusation.

Her demeanor softened and she came to my side, pressing her forehead against my shoulder. "I'm sorry, Michael." She looked up and her eyes were wet with new tears. "My father loves me. He wears this ring with three diamonds, one for each of his daughters, because he says we're his jewels. And I love my father. He came from a hard life, like you, and he's had to overcome a lot to get to where he is today and shelter us from the insecurities he felt as a child. That makes him worthy of my respect, but it doesn't make him right about you. If anything, he should better understand that it's the man inside that matters. But he can't see past his own struggles and he doesn't want us to experience them. My father worships money as the God that delivers us from our problems. As good a man as he is, he judges people, including himself, by their account balances.

"I love you, not for the things you have, or even what you might have or might become someday—but because of who you are right now and how you make me feel. I love the goodness of your heart. I have friends who have married rich boys with poor hearts and I pity them, in their new cars and big new homes, for all their poverty."

She looked down, and when her head rose again her face had changed as if in bitter acceptance of a fate she could not control. Her voice was more statement than it was pleading. "I will always love you. But I will not wait forever. Not because I won't, but because I can't . . ."

I looked down, avoiding her tearful gaze. She wiped her eyes with her hand, then walked toward the door. As I watched her go it was like one of those dreams where you open your mouth to scream but you can't. Then a voice inside of me said to let her go—that if I really loved her, I would let her find something better, something whole and new that she could build a real life around. And then something desperate screamed to me to hold on to her, to drag her back, that this might be my last chance. And while the voices fought, the front door shut behind her without my ever saying a word.

chapter thirteen

A Drawer of Letters

"It is folly, I suspect, to commence each morning with a letter to my lost love and conclude it with my diary, thereby bleeding at both ends of the day."

Excerpt from Esther Huish's Diary

By midmorning of the next day, most of the residents had returned from their Christmas visits. The Arcadia bustled in receiving them and settling them back into their diets, schedules, and routines. In one regard it was a godsend, as my absorption in work helped choke down my desperation over Faye. In the back of my mind I spent the better part of the day considering what I would say to her after work, until Sharon handed me a message from Faye canceling our date. She would be out with her family, the note read.

I had not had a chance to see Esther until

fifteen minutes before the end of my shift, and as I now had no plans for the evening, I decided to visit with her for a while. I looked forward to having someone to talk to. I walked into her room carrying the news-paper.

"Sorry I'm so late. It's been a madhouse around here."

"Are you off at five?" she asked.

"Yes, but it doesn't matter. I don't have any plans for tonight."

She seemed pleased. "Christmas Eve was lovely," she said gently. "Thank you for sharing it with me."

"You're welcome."

"You finally got time with Faye?"

"We spent yesterday together." I sighed. "The day couldn't have gone much worse. We got into a fight."

"Over what?"

"She was expecting a ring."

Esther's brow furrowed in concern. "Have you made up with her?"

"I had hoped to tonight. We had a date planned, but she called and canceled. I guess she's still pretty upset." I shook my head. "I don't know what I would have said anyway." I lifted the paper, eager to change the subject. "Ready for the obituaries?"

She nodded and I commenced, though she seemed especially contemplative and I wondered if she had even been listening. When I finished reading the day's passings, she spoke.

"You can't let her leave without speaking to her."

"I didn't plan to. But I may not have a choice in the matter."

"You must go to her," she said forcefully. "What if you don't get a second chance?"

I did not reply and she turned away, becoming more reflective. She seemed to be thinking about something, wavering over a decision. Then she said, "Michael, open the bottom drawer of my bureau."

There was no mistaking the gravity of her directive, and I looked at her quizzically, then squatted down. I grabbed a handle with one hand and lightly tugged. The drawer did not budge. I grasped its handles more firmly with both hands, then jerked it open. To my astonishment the entire drawer was filled with envelopes of different sizes and shapes, some yellowed with age. It looked like a post office sorting bin. Most peculiar was that there were no visible stamps or postmarks on any of the envelopes. Her letters, I thought.

I was about to push the drawer shut again when Esther said, "Read one."

I glanced back at her apprehensively. "You don't need to do this."

"They should be read."

I extracted one of the letters and unfolded it. I read the letter aloud.

My beloved Thomas,

Not a day passes that I do not think of you or wonder how different things might have been. I can only hope that life has been good to you, that your wife has brought you joy and love.

You are always in my heart,
Esther

I returned it to the drawer.

"Read another one," she said.

I reached into the pile and randomly selected another.

My beloved Thomas,

Today is a difficult day. It is like all the other difficult days, when I find myself en-

closed by walls of regret and self-disdain and it is all I can do to not run to you, to beg you to somehow take me back. To give my whole self to you is all I desire, but all that is left me is to punish the woman who let you go.

You are always in my heart,
Esther

Esther's head was bowed and I could not discern the effect this was having on her. I returned the pieces, wondering if it was possible that these hundreds of unsent letters could all be to the same man. How many hours had been spent in the penning or tears dropped over those words?

"Are they all to Thomas?"

"My soldier," she said. Almost instinctively her hand rose to the locket. Then, unexpectedly, she said, "He is still alive."

"Alive?"

"I saw him once. It was seventeen years ago at the county fair."

"It must have been a grand reunion."

"He did not see me. I only saw him."

"But certainly you went to him . . ."

She did not answer, and her old eyes blinked slowly. I came back to her side and sat down. "Esther. Why did you not marry the soldier?"

In truth I expected Esther to defer the query, to ask me about Faye or my scholarship or tomorrow's meal selection, for that matter. What I did not expect was the answer that followed.

chapter fourteen

Thomas

"A handsome young man came this evening to inquire for lodging, his intent being to stay in Betheltown for some while. I must remind myself that sunsets too are beautiful, before they leave you cold, dark, and alone."

Excerpt from Esther Huish's Diary

"My father was old when I was born. I'm not sure exactly how old—past sixty at least. My mother was only seventeen, and it was quite a scandal in the small town of Rexburg, Idaho—even in those days. After my mother died from complications of childbirth, we left Rexburg, traveling all over the mountain states, floating from job to job. We came to Betheltown when I was sixteen. It was before the Depression turned Bethel into a thriving town. We were accustomed to foraging for a living, and my father thought panning might be just as fruitful as begging for labor. It was three years later that the market crashed and the mines of Bethel began to reopen.

"When my father's health began to fail, I went to work at the Bethel Boarding House and Inn. I was one of only a few women in the mining camp, and the only one of youth. I was regularly courted by men." Esther spoke with fondness. "I cannot complain of the miners; as a whole they treated me like a community treasure. All one had to do to ensure a busted nose was to speak ill of me." She laughed, but then a shadow crossed her face. Her voice fell to match. "I was twenty when I met Frank. He was a miner from Topeka. He was burly and handsome and brought me flowers and sometimes taffy from Salt Lake City. He was very charming, I suppose. Or maybe I was just lonely. Except for my father, I had no one. Frank and I were married only six weeks after we met, and I was in a family way only six weeks later. With Matthew."

"I remember," I said. "Matthew was . . ."

"Matthew was retarded," she finished, as if accustomed to others' discomfort with the word. "Frank wouldn't accept Matthew as his son. At first he accused me of lying with another man. He knew it wasn't true, but it didn't matter. He was ashamed of his son." She repeated with disgust, ". . . ashamed of his own son. He would not let me carry Matthew in public. He would not even call him by name. It was always 'Boy.' Frank was mean. He was not the man I thought I had married, and I grew afraid of him. I would have left him, but I had my father and Matthew . . ." Esther spoke as if still attempting to justify past decisions.

"Frank treated me cruelly. I was not allowed to attend to my son or father until all of my husband's needs were met. He was harsh to my father as well. He never beat him, but he would humiliate him. My father was afraid of him. Frank was a big man and he liked to fight. He would stare down my father and I would submit to whatever Frank wanted so that he wouldn't hurt him. Even Matthew learned to hide whenever he came in the house.

"I thought that maybe if I were a better wife he would become kinder. For a while I blamed myself for giving him a retarded child. But things never got better. Frank was cruel. And he grew meaner and lazier. After three years he stopped working altogether and took to drinking all day, and when I didn't have money to give him to drink, he would scream for all to hear that it was because of the two retards that lived with us. Sometimes he would make me borrow for him to drink. Then Frank took to hanging out in Goldstrike for days at a time. Goldstrike wasn't like Bethel. It was a wicked town. Frank said he had work there, but he never once came back with money in his pockets. One day he just never came back. I heard later that he had been shot by a jealous husband. I guess it's better to be fast than big." She bowed her head. "I know it is terrible, but I was glad when I heard of his death. I thanked God."

"When did you meet Thomas?"

"Thomas came three years later. I thought a man would never be beautiful to me again. But I was wrong. He was the most beautiful man I had ever seen."

Esther seemed suddenly enveloped by memory and she shared her story with such completeness of heart that it was not difficult to imagine Esther and Thomas's first meeting.

Fifty years previously. Bethel, Utah, circa 1938

As day stole quietly beneath the pilfering shadows of dusk, leaving the Oquirrhs damp in the glow of a harvest moon, a rusted Ford T wagon with a wood-planked flatbed rumbled up the pocked dirt roadway that led to Bethel. In previous seasons the road was a creek bed, and now, without runoff, it was the principal route into the remote mining town. Thomas lay back against his canvas duffel on the truck's bed, facing the dust cloud that followed them and the eastern horizon that gradiated into dusk. He was dressed in an open wool overcoat and the spring air brushed his tousled hair forward, chill with the trace of winter's recent desertion and filled with the night's cacophony—the barking of foxes and the relentless symphonies of the locust. He turned and looked ahead through the cab as the shadow of a pitched, two-story adobe building, surrounded by a white picket fence, came to view. Thomas rapped his knuckles on the tin cab and the driver strained to look back.

"Up ahead's fine," he said, gesturing toward the structure. The man pulled the sputtering truck up to the inn and braked.

Thomas swung himself from the bed, hauled off his duffel, then peered into the cab at the truck's driver. "I hear they're gonna start magnetizing the rear axles on these jalopies."

"What's the idea?"

"Pick up the parts that fall off along the way."

The man smiled. "Yeah, but you can't kill the damn things with a Winchester."

Thomas slapped the tin hood. "Thanks for the ride, fellah."

"Name's Jed. You strike the mother lode, you remember that name." At this he laughed. "You ever seen raw gold?"

Thomas shook his head. "No."

"Didn't think so," he said in obvious amusement. He pushed down on the accelerator and the truck sputtered off.

Thomas surveyed the old inn, passed through the yard gate down a pebble rock path, climbed the porch, and entered the front door. The room was wide, with a half dozen tables vacant of humanity but for a gray-bearded man dozing in a chair near the entry. The door had barely shut behind Thomas when a young lady emerged from a back room. She wore awkward wire-rimmed glasses with curves that masked the perfect symmetry of her delicately shaped face and the high flushed cheeks on which the glass lenses rested. She was fair of feature, with dishwater hair and long eyelashes beneath lush brows that appeared altogether masculine—a paradox, Thomas thought. She was petite but appeared strong, as one who dwells in such environments must—yet her countenance had not assimilated the harshness of the terrain or her life. Though penuriously attired, she was handsome by nature and continued to turn many miners' heads, which she found more a nuisance than an asset—as irrelevant to her circumstances as a farmer might find the aesthetics of a farm implement.

Thomas tipped his hat. "Ma'am."

"What may I get you?" she asked, then added, "I'm done cooking for the evening."

"I need a place to stay awhile. Have you a bed?"

As she examined the stranger more closely, she felt the sudden and unwelcome stirrings of attraction. "We have a bed upstairs."

"Don't much care where it's at, long as it's under a roof."

"That's about all it has."

He reached for his pouch. "How much?"

"Thirty cents a day. Includes supper and breakfast."

"How much for a month?"

"That depends on how many days are in the month."

Thomas fished out some silver coins. "There's a week."

She took the coins, then took a key from her blouse pocket. "Room's up the stairway. Last one down the hall. Bedding's in the chest of drawers."

As Thomas took the key from her she no-

ticed how callused from labor her slender
hands had become and she was embarrassed, surprising herself with a rare display
of vanity. He noticed her discomfort.

"You mentioned supper."

"I serve at sundown. There's a few biscuits
left and some acorn pie. Neither's hot. For a
nickel I could heat up some coffee."

"I haven't eaten since Salt Lake. Pie and
coffee would be good."

"Just sit over at that table and I'll get it."

Thomas walked to the table, flung his
bag from his back, and stretched his legs
before the fire. He had been on the road for
a fortnight, had come nearly two thousand
miles, by train and foot, had witnessed
firsthand the desperation of a country
squirming beneath the heavy foot of the
Depression.

The woman returned, set the cup, plate,
and fork on the table before him, purposely
avoiding eye contact with the stranger.

"May I ask your name?"

She looked up, brushing back a single
strand of hair. For the only young woman in
a mining camp, it was not an infrequent inquiry, though usually intoned by lecherous
old men with chipped or absent teeth. It

sounded different from a lecherous young one, she thought.

"My name is Esther."

"You look tired. Why don't you join me for a spell?"

"I've still chores to do."

He gestured to the chair across the table from him. "Just for a spell. It would be real nice to talk with someone."

She gazed at him circumspectly; then, against her better judgment, she relented, pulled back the chair, and sat on its edge.

"How many residents do you bake for?"

"About sixty."

"Place doesn't look that big. Unless you're sleeping five to a bed."

"The miners stop here on the way to the mines." She added shyly, "They like my cooking."

He lifted a forkful of the pie.

"What mine did you come for?"

"What makes you sure I'm a miner?"

"If you're in Bethel you're either a miner or a gambler, and you don't dress well enough to be a gambler. At least one worth his salt."

"I didn't come to work for any mine. I'm doing my own prospecting."

"Then you are a gambler."

Thomas grinned. "I suppose so, ma'am."

"Why Bethel?"

"I've got myself a gold map."

"A map?"

"My father sent it a few years back. Before he died."

"Is it any good?"

"If it's anything like my father, it's worthless. But maybe the old man was trying to redeem himself."

"A gold map. I've never heard that one. How'd he come by it?"

"He wrote in a letter that he met a man who once served in Johnston's army around the time of the Utah war. Johnston hated the Mormons and thought, next to killing them, the best way to rid himself of them was by bringing outsiders to the Utah Territory. The surest way to do that was to find gold, or convince people that you had. So he encouraged his soldiers to prospect in their off time. This soldier was out prospecting when he found a ledge of quartz speckled with gold. It was getting dark, so he filled a pouch with gold nuggets, carved his initial into the bark of several of the nearby trees, and descended to camp. The next morning his unit raided an Indian camp and the soldier was killed in the skirmish. As he lay dying he told a comrade about his find and gave him the pouch of gold as proof. That's who my father met."

"Why didn't the soldier go after the gold himself?"

"On account he went AWOL. The massacre was a pretty bad thing. Soldiers killed everyone, old men, women with their babes in arms. He couldn't stomach the blood anymore. He just up and left the cavalry and went back east. Wrote the directions to the gold down in his diary."

"Why didn't your father just find the gold himself and send money?"

"He tried. But when he met the man he already had the consumption for a good while, and didn't go after it until his end was near. I don't know what drove him to look for the gold when he knew he was dying, but I don't count any of his ways as worth figuring."

"Gold does that to men. Avarice gets in a man's blood and he's willing to let a lot of things go," she said quietly. Thomas drank from his cup and guessed that there was something to what she had just said.

"What's your father's name?" she asked.

"Abrahm. Why?"

"It's a small town. Someone around will remember him."

Thomas looked displeased with the remark. "So, what's your story?"

"What makes you think I have one?"

"You're here."

"You say that as if it requires explanation."

"It begs explanation."

"I find that tremendously arrogant."

"How so?"

"It assumes that someplace else is better. Well, bigger isn't better, and I've yet to hear a convincing argument otherwise. I've heard men boast their town is better because it has more shootings than others."

Thomas smiled because he knew she was right. "Still, there is much you miss in a mining camp."

"Like last autumn's outbreak of influenza."

Thomas laughed. "And theater. Art shows. Fairs. Talkies. Dances."

"There are dances every Friday in Goldstrike," Esther said, despite the fact that she had never been to one.

"Have you ever lived in a big town?"

"Only as a child. If you consider Rexburg big."

"Then how do you know it's not superior?"

"One needn't sleep in an orchard to know what its fruit is like."

"And you found bad fruit?"

Esther's countenance changed and she suddenly stood. "That'll be a nickel for the coffee."

Thomas thought to apologize but wasn't certain on what account, so he just handed her the coin. She glanced once more at him before she disappeared into the kitchen. Thomas sat back in his chair, weary from the day's journey and disappointed to have lost her company. It had been a long while since he had shared in pleasant conversation with a female, and it looked now as though it would be a great deal longer before he would have more. The room's only sounds were the sputtering of the fire and the wheezing of the old man, who still sat motionless in the chair. When he finished his pie, he pushed back from the table, hoisted his bag over his shoulder, and ascended the stairwell to his new home.

I lay back onto Esther's bed, contemplating the tale. "Did he ever find the gold?"

She blinked successively. "No. He never did," she said despondently. "He searched every day until the next winter, then foraged around for years after that, but he never found it. It became a joke around Bethel. 'Ricorsi's gold,' they called it. Some thought it was one last fool trick his father played him for, but Thomas never gave in for that. Gold is a slippery thing.

"When his money started to wane, he hired on at the Fletcher mine. He kept his room at the boardinghouse, and so I saw him every day. He was always a gentleman. My father's health had deteriorated until he was bed bound, and Thomas stepped in, helping me with things around the place. He wouldn't take it from his board; he never asked for anything." Esther's eyes wet. "I knew he was different. Though he kept searching for his father's gold, I realized that he wasn't looking for gold at all. He was looking for something less tangible—perhaps a confirmation of his father's attempt to find forgiveness from his son.

"I saw this more clearly as he gradually spent more time with Matthew than looking for that gold. He'd take him to the ponds and teach him to fish. Showed him how to pan." A reminiscent smile crept across Esther's face. "Matthew came back once with a nugget worth at least five dollars. Of course, Thomas had put it there, but he denied it. Matthew bought himself an all-day sucker and me a bonnet, and we put the rest aside. That was how Thomas was. He lived humbly and shared generously. Only time he ever went to Goldstrike was for mail or provisions, and he'd always ask if he could bring me something back and I'd decline, then he'd bring back something special anyway.

"Still, I shunned his advances. As foolish as that sounds, Frank had left deep wounds. But Thomas persevered. Thomas wasn't shy, but he wasn't aggressive either. I suspect he was just waiting around for me to come to my senses. I don't know if the man had the patience of Job or the faith of Moses, but he never gave up." She looked down. "Then the war came.

"War was a long ways from Betheltown. Hitler, the Sudetenland, Dunkirk—they were just words thrown around Sunday-night conversations by the fireplace by men who did not have dishes to wash. They had no place in my life. Until they had place in my Thomas's. It had taken nearly three weeks for the draft notice to catch up to Thomas, and when it came he had less than two weeks to report to the Fort Douglas embark station in Salt Lake City and take the train to Fort Leonard Wood in Missouri.

"They were hard weeks. Thomas became pensive. Usually when someone is going to go away, they become anxious and peevish. Thomas wasn't that way. He became sweeter to me, not to get something, but as if he wanted to leave me something. I would be cleaning up at night and glance around and find him sitting alone just staring at me, not with his usual smile, but with an intensity that should have made me uncomfortable, but didn't. He was worried about me. Wondering about who would take care of Matthew and me. Even Matthew sensed it, I think. But there were other changes. I think during that time he found what he had come to Betheltown for."

"Love?"

"Something akin to it. Forgiveness. I think he came to peace with his own father." Esther held a tissue up to her nose.

"As his departure neared, I just felt more confused. He had made it so convenient for me, to have him where it was comfortable for me. I was churlish to him. I suppose I could feel a heartache coming and had no place for it. I had built such thick walls around my heart and only then did I realize that he had gotten inside of them, and it made me vulnerable."

I thought about Faye's departure and understood her words.

"Thomas asked if he might spend some time with me the night before he was to leave. He came late that night, after the dinner was gone and the miners had gone to their rooms. We were alone together in the dining room and we sat by the fire and hardly said a thing. I remember watching the fire dance in his eyes and wondering, how a man could be so beautiful. Then he turned and said, 'It's just not right.' I asked, 'What's not right?' and then he brought out this velvet pouch and took from it a locket. This very one," she said, touching the piece.

"I had no fine jewelry, and as I held it, he told me that it had belonged to his mother. That it was gold, but she had it plated in silver to smuggle it out of the old country. He said he thought maybe it would remind me of him, and maybe there was something to the more precious metal being beneath. It had his picture inside and he had inscribed on the back, *Always, Thomas.* He put it around my neck.

"I was speechless. A part of me wanted to dissolve into him, but I knew that if I did, I would never get myself back. Then he spilled from that pouch a ring. It was the most beautiful ring I have ever seen. It was a golden band with a dark emerald stone. He said, 'I've no right to ask a woman to take a man that may not be coming back . . . but if I'm not to return, it would be wrong for a woman to not at least know how he felt.' He held the ring out to me and gazed at me for the longest time, but I couldn't touch it. I was too afraid to let him take what was left of me. I was too afraid. I just couldn't touch it. I began to sob, and he just looked at me, and then he turned away and there were tears running down his face, and he threw the ring in the fire and walked out of the room."

Esther turned suddenly quiet and I knew that she had gone deep inside herself to share this story. But it was a journey that she had not made for herself. It was neither indulgent nor painless, any more than removing a bandage to examine a wound. I was certain that it was an act performed solely for my benefit, if I were wise enough to learn from her scars. It was dark outside when she finished, and I glanced down at my watch, then gently touched her arm. "I better go," I said softly. "I need to call Faye."

She nodded in understanding. I stood, and as I looked back at her I suddenly felt a pang of guilt, as she had just laid wide open her heart and it seemed wrong to leave her alone and vulnerable. "Will you be okay?"

"Go to Faye," she said.

"Then I'll see you tomorrow."

"Tomorrow will be better," she said.

As I drove home, my mind replayed Esther's story of love's loss. I had vividly imagined Betheltown from her description, and Esther and Thomas kneeling at the hearthside with broken hearts and uncertain futures. Her tale raised as many questions as it answered, and as many questions about myself as Esther. I set it all aside the moment I arrived home, intent on my own challenges of love. I laid my coat across the couch and dialed Faye's number.

"Hello, Michael."

"Hi, Abby. Is Faye home?"

"Yeah," she awkwardly replied. "Just a moment."

A hand cupped the mouthpiece and I could hear a brief, muffled altercation, then a hostile voice boomed over the phone.

"This is Dr. Murrow. Clearly you didn't get my drift the other night, so let me put it more succinctly. Stay the hell away from my daughter. She has more to worry about right now than a loser like you."

"I need to speak with her."

"She doesn't want to talk to you."

"Then let her tell me that. All she has to do is tell me that, and you'll never have to worry about me again."

He slammed down the phone. I threw the receiver across the room. I put my coat back on with the intent of driving over to her house, knowing full well that I was risking a violent confrontation. It would not be the first time I had to fight for something I cared about. I paused in my doorway for a moment, then, instead, went to the kitchen and made some tea to calm myself down. I was not deterred by her father or by confrontation, but by Faye herself. Frankly, I did not know how she would respond to my gesture. I could withstand her father's assaults, but I could not face her rejection.

chapter fifteen

Forgiveness

"There are those who clutch to resentment like it were a treasure of great worth. This is foolishness. The question to be asked is not how badly we were wronged, but what are we profited by our unforgiveness?"

Excerpt from Esther Huish's Diary

During my first quarter at the university, I had attended a lecture by a philosophy professor advancing the proposition that our concept of God is analogous to our perception of our own father. I found the theory personally intriguing, as I had been thirteen years old, huddled in blankets in the laid-down flat of a Chrysler station wagon, when I decided that there was no God. My mother and I were fleeing Wyoming and the alcoholic father who had abandoned us. My atheism has waned with time, passing through shades of agnosticism into the warmth of belief, due, in no small part, to my mother's faith.

* * *

I suppose I have always had problems with fathers, and Dr. Murrow was simply the most recent in a long line of hostile patriarchs. He was manic enough that I knew it would be futile to attempt phoning his home again while he was still there, so I waited until I arrived at the Arcadia to make the call, though I hoped that Faye would call first. She never did, and her silence burst loudly through my shell-shocked heart. It was only after my call that I began to understand just how deeply Faye had been hurt. Jayne answered the telephone.

"Hello, Michael," she said brightly.

"Hi. What are you doing home from school?"

"I'm still on Christmas break."

"Of course. Is Faye there?"

"No, she's gone with my parents to Salt Lake."

"When will she be back?"

"Not until late."

I was dismayed by the news.

"I'm sorry about what happened last night," Jayne added. "It's like my dad has become psychotic."

"How is Faye?"

She hesitated. "I've never seen her so up-set before."

"Would you ask her to call me when she gets back? I don't care how late it is."

"I don't know if she will, Michael. I don't know what you said to her, but you really broke her heart."

"Will you tell her that I love her and I'm sorry?"

"I will."

"You're a sweetheart."

"I miss having you around. You two have got to get back together."

"I'm trying, Jayne."

"Bye, Michael. I hope to see you soon."

I could only hope.

The Arcadia was not quite as harried as the previous day, and Helen set me to removing three floors of Christmas decorations, an act that entertained a small group of residents who followed me from bough to garland and applauded briefly when I brought down the star from the dayroom's plastic tree. I had spent the day detached from my surround-ings, immersed in my thoughts of Faye. If the doctor had planned to keep Faye from seeing me, he had done well, though I could not dismiss Faye's collaboration. I knew her well enough to know that she would not stay away if she didn't want to.

Despite my anxiety, Faye was not the only woman on my mind. The previous night's discussion with Esther continued to weave itself throughout my thoughts, as if to bind her plight with mine into a single tapestry. I had questions for her and I purposely planned to visit her at shift's end, when there would be time. When I arrived she was eager to talk with me.

"Did you make up with Faye?" she asked hopefully.

"No. I haven't even seen her. Her father pretty much has her sequestered."

"Will she leave tomorrow?"

"Tomorrow morning," I said dolefully.

Esther's forehead wrinkled.

"It's always the father. It starts out well enough, then they start asking questions."

"It's a shame," Esther said.

"I've wondered at times how different my life would be had I grown up with a real father."

"I have wondered the same about my mother. My father tried to fill her absence, but it's not the same. Even at my age I still consider what my life might have been like with her."

"What was your father like?"

She sighed. "Oh, he was a timid man. Miners used to say he looked like an emaciated version of Herbert Hoover. I suppose he was just about as popular. With my mother gone we traveled constantly, always chasing an easy dollar. He was a fool and a schemer, but he was always scheming on my behalf. He never forsook that responsibility for me. Now that I'm old, I understand that, and I love him for that. Not that I'm any wiser, just that old age lends perspective. And that leads to forgiveness."

"I couldn't say that about my father," I said tersely. "I will never forgive him."

She looked disturbed by my comment. "You say that as if forgiveness was a gift you were giving to him."

"Isn't it?"

"Your father's dead. What could forgiveness possibly profit him?"

I could not answer her question. "You think that I should forgive my father?" I asked incredulously.

"You must forgive him if you are ever to be free of him. We are chained to that which we do not forgive."

"I'm not chained to my father," I asserted.

"Far more than you know, apparently. Imagine a ship trying to set sail while towing an anchor. Cutting free is not a gift to the anchor. You must release that burden, not because the anchor is worthy, but because the ship is."

I thought of my father and immediately felt the blackness that enveloped all memory of him. "I don't know if I could forgive him for abandoning us. Even if I wanted to."

"Anyone can forgive if they will make the decision to. It may not come all at once, as resentment is a habit and must be coaxed from the heart. But with time it will come. You must pray for it. You must pray for the unforgiven."

"It would seem that forgiving him would be a betrayal of my mother."

"Would it please your mother to know that you were filled with hate?"

The question left me speechless.

"Sometimes forgiveness comes with understanding. Have you ever considered why he left?"

"I know why he left. He loved his booze more than his family."

"You cannot be certain of that. Your father could not control his drinking. He may have been weak, or chose to give in to his weaknesses, but where did that leave him?"

"They found him dead next to a Dumpster behind a hamburger joint."

"Why would he go to the streets when he could have stayed where he was warm and safe?"

"What are you implying?"

"I don't know your father. Maybe he was a demon. But I knew my first husband. He drank constantly. He left Matthew and me alone every chance he could, but he was always sure to come back for more money . . . or whatever else he craved. As pathetic a man as you think your father was, he may have been honest enough with himself to know that he was too weak to ever change. It is possible that your father left to free you and your mother. Is there another explanation?"

Again I could not answer her.

"You must search for forgiveness, Michael. It is not unlike Thomas's search and the peace he eventually found."

"But Thomas never found his father's gold. There was no justification for him to believe that his father was trying to make good."

"Perhaps. But he did find peace."

I considered her words, then pushed them forward to a different conversation. A more comfortable one. "There's one thing I don't understand. Why you didn't go to Thomas when you saw him years later."

"It was not so simple," she said sadly.

"Did you ever hear from him again after that night by the fireplace?"

She nodded, but said nothing.

"What happened after Thomas left?"

My prodding seemed to re-open the lid on that box of grievous memories and Esther turned sullen and began rocking in her chair. After a minute she sighed, then began to speak.

"I didn't sleep that night. I heard him come back a few hours later and go to his room. Then I heard him leave again. The next morning I combed through the fireplace cinders until I found the ring. The ring was there. But he was gone. He packed his things and left in the night." She sighed. "At first I thought my feelings would just wane with time, but they didn't. I thought about him every day. I worried that he would be killed in the war, then I wondered how I would even know if he was. I didn't know where he was, he had left in such a hurry. Most of all I wondered if he would ever return to Betheltown." Her words fell off in sadness. She touched the corner of her eye.

"After almost two years I just gradually stopped wondering. There was nothing in it. Betheltown was dying and everyone was leaving. Matthew and I had nothing else, no place else to go, so we just cared for the inn. We were down to a handful of boarders, and half of those couldn't pay any rent, so they helped with chores or kept a garden. We lived together communally and we just slowly died with the town. It was two years to the day that Thomas left that I was married to one of the boarders. His name was William. It wasn't a marriage of love—there was no pretense of that. It was of convenience and loneliness. William didn't know why I chose the day I did. To him it didn't matter much. William was a lot older than me. He wasn't the brightest man, but he was good and he accepted Matthew. I suppose he knew that I didn't love him, but he accepted that too. I fulfilled the companionship he needed, and in a way, he fulfilled mine and Matthew's.

"A few years later, the last of the mines closed and Betheltown died. We had some money, not a lot by any account, but enough to start somewhere else, so we picked up and went to Salt Lake City. We lived in a little trailer near Millcreek Canyon and for a while we were content. It wasn't the life I would have hoped for, the kind that little girls dream about, but perhaps the best I could expect. The Depression and the war were over, and it seemed that days of prosperity had finally come. There was a place for Matthew to play and regular church every Sunday at a Baptist chapel. I didn't forget Thomas. Not a day went by that I didn't think of him. But I had put him in a place that was somehow safe, out of view, but still there if I needed to touch it, like the ring he gave me. I never took the locket off. William never asked about it, though I suspected it hurt him.

"One day, as unexpected as a summer rain shower, Thomas came back. I was doing the dishes when Matthew came running into the house breathless and smiling. 'Tom,' he said. He remembered him. I toweled off my hands and went outside, and he was there—outside my gate. He was changed some, huskier in the shoulders, and he wore those thick-framed glasses that were in style." She smiled in remembrance. "He looked older, but not much. He had come back from Europe only a month before, and it took him a while to make his way west. He had been to Betheltown and found it dead, and it had taken him nearly a month to hunt me down. William wasn't around that day; he had gone off into the city for business. I invited Thomas to sit down and have some lemonade. I asked him about the war but he didn't want to talk about it. He had seen the living dead of Buchenwald and many more just dead, and said it wasn't exciting like the newsreels made it out to be, that it was just filled with hatred and death and stench, but it was done and Hitler was dead and that was good. He kept glancing at the ring on my hand, but he wouldn't ask, and it took me a good hour to speak of William. When I finally did, something seemed to die inside of him, right there in front of me. He went real quiet after that, and then he kissed me and said he had to go.

"I asked him where he was going and he said he reckoned he'd settle in the valley and he'd write and let me know. He got a job out at the Magna copper mines, between Salt Lake and Bethel. Worked his way up to the smelters, got himself in with the unions. People trusted Thomas. He cared about people. Not like some say because they want you to think them good, but he just did, like it was a natural thing." She paused for a moment, then said, "Kind of like you, Michael. There is much of Thomas to you."

I could not think of a nicer compliment. "Thank you," I replied simply.

"About four years later, William just up and died. It was a stomach ailment. Doctors said he had bad blood. Truth be told, I don't think anyone really knew what it was. He just groaned loudly one day and then he started in with a fever, and sometime in the night he died. He had been buried only a week when I took the car and went to find Thomas."

"But you didn't find him?"

"I went to the city of Magna. It's not a big town, and a woman at a butcher's shop showed me the way to Thomas's. Gave me his address. I parked across the street and walked up to his home. There was a little girl playing in the yard. She had long dark hair. She was the prettiest little thing. She looked just like my Thomas. Over the fence I asked her name. She said, 'Katelyn Ricorsi.' I asked her who her father was and she said, 'Mr. Tom Ricorsi.' I looked up and then I saw the woman standing on the porch. She was beautiful. She had long brown hair and the most pleasant smile. She asked if she could help me, if maybe I was looking for someone. I asked her name and she took my hand and said, 'Martha Ricorsi, pleased to know you.' The little girl came and put her arms around her mama's legs. She said I must be a stranger because everyone out that way knew each other and she asked again if she could help me find someplace. I just stared at them for the longest time without answering, and then I said no, I was sure I had the wrong street. I got back in the car and went home." Esther bowed her head. "I wrote my first letter to Thomas that day. I knew I could never send it. What did that woman or that little girl ever do to me? All Martha Ricorsi ever did was love a man who deserved to be loved. I had my chance."

"And you have never spoken to him?"

"There has not been a day since that I have not thought of him. But I never spoke to him again." I noticed a single tear. "I came down with the scarlet fever that next fall. That's when Matthew died. I have been alone ever since."

In the outer hall I could hear the electric undulations of the commercial floor polisher as it passed down the darkened corridor, and Esther sat quietly in her chair, slowly swaying back and forth, and her voice came soft and weary. "That is why I follow the obituaries. Maybe there will be a second chance."

I suddenly understood the daily ritual. "Maybe there will." I covered my mouth to yawn, then checked my watch. "It's late. I better go." I kissed her forehead, then stood.

"Sleep well. You will go to Faye?"

"I'll see her at the airport."

Even though Esther and Faye had never met, Esther said, "Say good-bye for me."

I took her hand. "I'll do that."

As I drove home that night, the forsaken roads indulged the glow of a crescent moon, and I thought of Esther and the loneliness and regret of her years, and then I thought of Faye, and it should have been clear to me what I needed to do. It ought to have been clear to me. To a better man it would have been.

chapter sixteen

The Departure

"There have been too many departures in my life. I have yet to find the good in good-bye or the well in farewell."

Excerpt from Esther Huish's Diary

I did not sleep that night. I woke continually to check the alarm and would find that only a half hour or so had passed from the last checking, and finally, at five-thirty, I just got up and read. Three hours later I made the drive to Salt Lake International. When I arrived at the terminal I checked for gates and found that Faye's flight was scheduled to leave twenty minutes earlier than I had thought. I frantically hurried through the crowded airport terminal. Faye was already near the front of the line, standing next to her father, waiting to board with the other first-class passengers, when I called to her.

She turned, and I could not read her expression. "Michael?"

Her father glared at me, and Faye touched his sleeve, then set down her bag and stepped out of line. She came and stood before me. Neither of us spoke for a moment, then Faye took a deep breath and took my hand. "I have never cried so much as I have the last few days, Michael."

I looked around uncomfortably. "I'm sorry, Faye." I took a deep breath. "It's just so complex."

"That's the problem, Michael. It's not."

I noticed that she was not wearing the locket I had given her. I reached into my pocket. "I want to give you something before you leave." I brought out a ring, a simple, thin smooth band of Black Hills gold. I pressed it into Faye's hand. "It was my mother's." Faye looked at it, then her eyes began to moisten and she handed it back. "I can't take it, Michael."

"Why?"

"That night . . ." She tried to continue but was overcome by emotion. She bit her lip as she struggled to gain her composure. Her father suddenly called out, "Come on, Faye. It's time to board."

Faye wiped her eyes, then covered her mouth with her hand. "I've got to go." She leaned forward and kissed my cheek. "Good-bye, Michael."

"Will you call me?"

Her head bowed, she took a few steps, then stopped and turned back to me. "I'll always love you" is all she said.

She returned to the line wiping her eyes, while her father stared hatefully at me. The attendant handed Faye her boarding pass and she slipped it into her blouse pocket, then squatted down and crossed her chest with the strap of her carry-on and lifted it. She glanced back at me once more, and we just looked into each other's eyes, then she turned away, disappearing into the jetway.

chapter seventeen

Auld Lang
Syne

"At the arrival of this new year I can only wonder if Thomas will return, though I fear the answer. There are those who will read the last page of a book first. But it is not me. I believe that it is fortunate that we are allowed to turn just one page of our lives at a time."

Excerpt from Esther Huish's Diary

Although I knew what to fear from Faye's departure, I was less certain of what to expect. The only thing I was sure of was that I had wounded her deeply.

The next two days passed with great effort, as if each minute had to be coaxed from a quagmire of melancholy. I busied myself with my work in an effort to elude the ache that seemed to wait around each thought. I was filling out residents' progress reports in the dayroom when one of the residents, Wally, hobbled toward me. He sported a canary yellow cardigan and bottle-glass-thick eyeglasses that magnified the milky irises of his cataracts. His pants were belted up around his ribs.

According to facility records, Wally's given name was Patrick, but I'm not certain that he would answer to it, as he had grown accustomed to his new moniker. The nickname was a product of evolution. In its genesis, it had started as Ralph Waldo, an allusion to the great essayist, as Wally had once been employed as a high school English teacher and noted for his fondness for spouting Emerson. Through the natural erosion of the epithet, "Wally" was all that survived.

In the course of his career he had memorized the better part of Emerson's works, then spent his aging years forgetting them piecemeal, leaving behind a tangled, yet still recitable, hodgepodge of misguided canons and crippled tenets. But what was lost in accuracy was made up for in earnestness, and he spoke with such fervor that those with whom he shared the damaged essays would likely believe that Wally was not in error, rather that Emerson did, occasionally, say truly peculiar things.

Wally's shadow crossed my paperwork.

"I'm dying, you know," he said abruptly.

I looked up from my work, regarding the remark with dubiousness. "Of what?"

He lowered himself onto the chair next to me, supporting his descent against the black wooden cane positioned between his bulbous knees. "Whatever gets me first, I suppose."

"You don't know what you're dying of?"

"No point in it. It's like caring about the color of the viper that bit you."

I went back to my paperwork.

"So what is it with you, anyway?" he asked.

"I'm just busy today, Wally," I said without looking up.

"You've been pining so thick you could cut through the gloom with a machete. I suspect there's a female on the other end of it."

I found his observation intriguing enough to interrupt my work.

"If you want the honest answer—"

"Don't want a dishonest one," he interjected.

"—my girlfriend's gone."

The old man gazed at me with a curious expression of amusement. "Young love," he muttered to himself. "Youth wouldn't know love if it were three hundred pounds and sitting on its chest."

I found the metaphor unpalatable.

"You want love, son, you got Nedward there." He pointed toward an old man across the room, feeble and hunchbacked, slumped back in a chair.

"There's Don Juan, all right," I said derisively.

Wally was annoyed by my observation, and the timbre of his voice changed from harlequin to sage.

"You don't know squat. You think love wears a young body and pretty face. That's a fool's mind. Nedward hobbles on bad knees a mile every day to hold the hand of a woman who no longer recognizes him." He looked carefully into my face. "Love doesn't get any more real than that."

Wally pushed himself erect, then slowly walked back to the other side of the room.

Esther did not ask about Faye, and I suppose she didn't need to. I assumed it an act of mercy on her part, though she spoke exceptionally gently and I suspect she was, in her way, just letting me know that she was ready to listen when I was ready to talk. Peculiarly, it was Alice who first broached the issue of Faye's departure.

"Are you okay?" she asked sweetly.

"I'm fine," I lied.

"Something happen between you and Faye?"

I was amazed by her perceptiveness. "We didn't part well."

"I'm sorry," Alice said sincerely. "Been there." She grinned sympathetically. "What time are you off tomorrow?"

"Six."

"What are you doing for New Year's Eve?"

"I thought I'd come around here and bang some bedpans."

Alice grinned. "Why don't you come with me to a New Year's Eve party?"

She sensed my reluctance. "It's not a date. We're just going to have a good time . . . or you could stay home and brood in the new year."

I grinned. "Okay."

"Want me to pick you up?"

"How about if I just meet you there?"

"If you promise you won't flake out." She picked up a health chart and penned an address on the back. "It's the Liss home, up near Thirtieth. We're starting at seven."

I checked the address. "I know the area. It's up near Faye's."

"Where the rich kids run," she confirmed.

I folded the paper and slid it into my breast pocket.

"Don't lose that," Alice said, pleased that I had relented. "And don't worry about bringing anything. We've got enough chips and beer for the millennium."

The Liss estate was about as difficult to find as the Empire State Building. It owned a good piece of the mountain, with backyard tennis courts, an indoor swimming pool, two Jacuzzis, and a game room the size of my home, replete with big-screen television, commercial pinball machines, and billiards. The stereo blasted Styx's *Equinox* as Alice met me in the spacious marble-floored foyer. She was dressed casually, in designer jeans and a low-cut tan silk blouse.

Alice had understated the libations, and the massive kitchen was stocked with immense amounts of consumables and large ice-filled tins with beer, wine coolers, and pop. We walked the grounds as Alice introduced me to her friends, each of whom offered me a drink, which, through years of practice, I adroitly declined. It wasn't long, however, before I became known as Alice's designated driver. It was a cordial gathering, as such events go, though there was a near fray in the game room, which was quickly aborted as the man's more sober date enticed him to another part of the house. At midnight a group began throwing one another into the indoor pool with their clothes on; most of them, I suspected, wanted to remove them anyway, and it was shortly after the new year was pronounced that couples began pairing off. Alice and I sat on the couch, eating pretzels and watching Dick Clark feign excitement in the Times Square revelry. Alice had carried a bottle in her hand all night and set it down only then to take my hand.

"Ever seen a place this big?"

"Never."

"Not even Faye's?"

"Her place isn't anything like this."

She stood, pulling me forward from the couch. "Come with me, I want to show you something." I followed her down a flight of shag-carpeted stairs to a long, darkened corridor. We stopped outside the last room of the hall—a bedroom.

"This is the place."

I looked into the vacant room. "This is what you wanted to show me?"

"No, this is *where* I wanted to show you." She began unbuttoning my shirt.

"Alice."

She smiled alluringly. "You don't like girls?"

"You've had too much to drink."

She put her finger on my nose. "Nope. You haven't had enough." She ran her finger down to my lips, then chin. "You know you're gorgeous."

"I'm not going to do this."

A broader smile spread across her face and I could smell the sweet pungency of the wine coolers on her breath. "Don't tell me that you're saving yourself for Faye."

"Something like that."

Alice laughed. "You think she's going to remember you after her first week in college? She may be a princess, but she's no saint." She resumed unbuttoning my shirt. "She sure as hell ain't saving anything for you."

I put my hand on hers. "I'm going to leave now, Alice."

She pressed up against me. "Come on. Don't you like the way I look?"

Of necessity I ignored the question. I put my hands on her waist to push her back, but didn't, and she smiled knowingly. Victoriously.

"Come on, Mikey," she said sweetly. "Faye's just another rich girl who wants you for the same reason all we girls do. But you know how it is. You're a great appetizer, but when it comes time to order, she's going to want the full course." She put her hands on mine and pulled them back farther around her waist, pressing her chest against mine. "Come on. I can make you forget her." She kissed my chin, then progressed to my neck, then leaned back, smiling enticingly. "I can make you want to forget her."

It was an effective seduction and I would be lying if I said that I wasn't tempted. But if my alarms of conscience were being systematically squelched by escalating desire, they were replaced by a new siren, louder and stronger perhaps than anything I had ever felt before, as my heart screamed out not just for love, but Faye's love.

I left Alice alone in the hall.

chapter eighteen

Second Chances

"That which we spend our lives hoping for is often no more than another chance to do what we should have done to begin with."

Excerpt from Esther Huish's Diary

The next morning Helen did not share my relief over Alice's sick call.

"No doubt she's still hungover from New Year's Eve," she grumbled as I took my smock from my locker. "I need you to follow up on her priority list. There are some things I need done this morning."

"I can do it," I assured her.

"Thank you. I know you can. By the way, Esther has been waiting impatiently for you. She has good news."

It was not the kind of pronouncement you expected about Esther.

"What good news?"

"Oddly enough, I think it has something to do with someone dying. She had me cut out the obituary."

I immediately climbed the stairs to Esther's room. I found her sitting on the edge of her bed, next to a red sequined clutch purse and a broad-rimmed hat. She wore a bright knit sweater. Her silver hair had been done up by one of the beauty schools that trained students on the residents' coifs, and her cheeks were garishly rouged as she had applied her makeup herself.

"Michael, is that you?" Her voice was steeped in excitement.

"You look like you're expecting someone," I said.

"Your arrival." She stood.

"What's the occasion?"

"My second chance." She felt around the bed until she found the clipped section of newspaper and handed it forward. I scanned the column.

"Thomas's wife died," I said.

"I don't mean to appear pleased for her passing . . ." Her voice coiled through the complexity of her emotions. ". . . She died last Wednesday. The funeral services were Friday afternoon."

I set the paper down, not sure of what to say.

"Will you take me to him?"

"Of course I will. We're shorthanded today; I don't think I can go until after my shift."

"Will you be through at five?"

"Yes."

She sat back down on the bed, her excitement somewhat cooled. "I've waited a lifetime already; another few hours won't hurt."

I took a tissue from an embroidered Kleenex holder. "Let me fix this. Looks like you got a little excited." I rubbed the lipstick away from her cheek. "There. You look beautiful."

She smiled, and her spirit was light as I left the room.

Helen let me off work a half hour early, and pocketing the obituary, I helped Esther on with her coat, then led her out to my car. We made our way to Thomas's.

Magna, Utah, lies about twenty miles due west of Salt Lake City, where the Oquirrh range dips into the Great Salt Lake. Magna was a copper mining town and its denizens were men of the trade, a melting pot of immigrants who came to work in the pit mine and its satellite smokestacked smelters. The town's name was not derived from its industry but from its Masonic founders, who borrowed the name from their code, *Magna est veritas, et praevalebit:* truth is mighty, and will prevail.

It is nearly an hour's drive from Ogden to the small town, and our journey was unusually silent. It was not for lack of thought. Esther's anxiety was palpable, and I would occasionally glance over and she would be smiling, lost in memory or dream, I mused; then I would turn back and she would seem apprehensive and tense. Ten minutes from the city limit, Esther asked, "What if he doesn't think I am pretty anymore? What if he just sees a decrepit old woman?" She pressed her palm against her forehead. "Of course, that is what he will see."

I glanced over at her, then reached over and took her hand. "You know, when my mother died, she had lost all her hair from the cancer treatments. She weighed less than eighty pounds. But all I could see was how beautiful she was."

Esther slowly digested my comment. "Thank you."

A few minutes later we slowed to a stop,

then turned south off the freeway onto an adjacent two-laned roadway.

"Are we in Magna?"

"Just about."

She took a deep breath. "You need to look at Thomas very closely for me, so you can afterward tell me everything about him. He is so handsome. His hair was beautiful. It was long and wavy. The kind of hair a woman loves to run her fingers through . . ."

I thought she spoke more like a love-struck teenager than an elderly woman, and I could not help but smile. I was glad that she was happy.

". . . I hope he hasn't lost all his hair. I don't mind if he has, of course—we're not spring chickens—but I hope that it is still long . . . of course, it won't be black any-more, but if it is long and beautiful silver." She laughed to herself. "I won't know the dif-ference. You could tell me it's black and I'd have no choice but to believe you. I wonder if he will let me run my fingers through it. I used to love to do that."

I turned west on the town's main street, cruised slowly its dusty drag. Magna was an infirm town, thought terminal by some, and more than half the buildings we passed were boarded up and awash in graffiti. Three blocks west I stopped to check a road sign, then progressed one more street and turned south up a pocked asphalt lane, scanning the addresses on the tired homes as I drove. I stopped in front of Thomas's.

It was a small, box-shaped house, which varied little from the others on the street. Each home had been erected fifty years previously, using the same blueprint, hammers, and mortgage company. The windows and front porch were shielded beneath striped white-and-green metal awnings, the bright green faded olive where exposed to the weather of a half century. I remembered Esther's story about the girl she had seen playing in the fenced yard. The wrought iron fence remained, though it was now old and rusted and overgrown with orange-berried pyracantha bushes. In the center of the front yard a naked chinaberry tree exposed a deserted bird's nest in its upper limbs.

"Are we there?" Esther asked, her voice tinged with anticipation.

"This is the place."

We sat motionless for a moment as she gathered herself.

"Are you ready?"

She nodded.

"I'll ring the bell first," I suggested. "Just to make sure he's there."

Esther did not object, so I walked up the weathered concrete path leading to the elevated stone porch and pressed the doorbell. A minute passed without result, so I pounded my fist against the wooden door. The door abruptly opened to a woman a generation older than myself, with a thin face and long black hair infiltrated with gray. She wore wide-framed designer glasses with tinted lenses.

"What can I do for you?" she asked with the brusqueness of one encountering a door-to-door salesman.

"Is this the Thomas Ricorsi home?"

"Yes," she answered guardedly.

"My name is Michael Keddington. I work at a nursing home in Ogden. One of our residents was a friend of Mr. Ricorsi's. She heard of his wife's passing and wished to pay her respects."

Her countenance relaxed. "Of course."

"Are you his daughter?"

She nodded. "I'm Kate." She looked over my shoulder to the street. "Is that the woman in the car?"

I nodded.

"Who is she?"

"Her name is Esther Huish. Perhaps your father has mentioned her."

"No. I'm sorry. But I live in southern California; I just came up for Mom's funeral."

"If it's all right, I'll get her. She's blind."

She glanced again at the car. "My father's taken my mother's death pretty hard. She probably shouldn't stay too long."

"I respect that. Thank you. This means a lot to her."

I walked back to the curb. Esther flinched as I grabbed the passenger door handle. "Have you seen him? Is he at the door?"

"His daughter answered the door. She said it's okay for us to visit for a minute."

Esther began wringing her hands. "Do I look presentable?"

"If I reach eighty I should hope to look so good," I quipped. "Let me help you out."

I took her arm and guided her up the cracked walkway to the porch while the woman held open the front door.

"Esther, this is Thomas's daughter, Kate."

"Hello, Kate."

"Mrs. Huish."

Esther paused next to her. "Have you any other brothers or sisters, Kate?"

"No. The family ended with me."

"Do you still have black hair?"

"What's left of it."

"We met once," Esther said. "But you would not recall it. You were just a little girl."

"I'm sorry, I don't recall."

As we entered the room Kate casually mentioned, "Esther is my middle name."

The living room was dim, its windows obscured by gaudy gold-ribbed curtains with gold-braided tassels. In the center of the room was a velour kidney-shaped couch fronting a matching pair of antiqued coffee tables adorned with Catholic icons. On the adjacent wall was a gold-leafed framed print of the Madonna with an exposed heart. The room smelled of basil from the cooking in the adjacent kitchen. Kate guided us down a short hallway to a small bedroom opposite the hall of the kitchen. She opened the door to reveal a man lying in bed beneath an ocher-hued wool blanket. He had lost much of his hair and what remained was uncombed, gathered in white wisps. His skin was olive and sun marked and unshaven, with white, spiky growth. His eyes were closed.

Kate spoke loudly. "Papa, you have a visitor."

The man's eyes slowly opened. "Huh?"

"You have a visitor. She is a friend of yours. Esther Huish."

I led Esther over to the side of the bed.

"Martha?" he rasped.

The woman squatted next to her father. "Papa, this isn't mama. This is a friend of yours."

He looked confused. "Where's Martha?"

The woman glanced back at me as if to say, "See how it is?" "Papa, this is Esther. Esther Huish."

The man did not respond.

"Could I be alone with him for a moment?" Esther asked.

We left the room and Kate walked back to the kitchen, while I lingered close to the bedroom door. From the kitchen came the sound of a metal spoon scraping a pan.

Esther knelt down next to the bed, and her trembling hand moved forward until she touched him. At first she just felt him without speaking. She softly caressed his face, savoring the flesh she had waited so long to touch. "Thomas. It's me, Esther."

He stared into her face with blank eyes. "Where's Martha?"

"She's gone, Thomas. She's died."

"Died?"

"Thomas, it's me. Esther."

He was silent for a moment, and I prayed fervently for the man's memory to come back—for the dimmest flicker of recognition. He suddenly bellowed, "I don't know you."

At his outburst I quietly opened the door. Esther felt across the man's body until she found his hand and took it in hers. She lifted it, pressed it to her cheek.

"Thomas, it's Esther . . . your darling, Esther."

The man said nothing, then turned to his side and began mumbling. A tear fell down Esther's cheek, then her body began to quake. She lowered her head into the bed and in a soft voice laden with grief she said, "I've waited a lifetime for you, Thomas. I've waited a lifetime."

I could not endure the scene any longer. I went in and crouched down next to her, laying my arm across her back. "Esther, let's go."

The man rolled toward us, jabbering incoherently.

Esther did not move, and I tightened my arm around her, pulling her into my shoulder. "Come on, Esther. We'll come back at a better time. Tomorrow. We'll come back tomorrow."

Her frail body began to shake. She could not speak at first, then, when she could, the voice came faint and hopeless. "I have no more tomorrows."

I did not know what to say. I suspect that there was nothing to say. Esther fell into my shoulder and wept.

chapter nineteen

Winter in
Arcadia

"Winter is difficult in Betheltown. But I believe it is God's plan that we suffer the cold of Winter that we might know the warmth of Spring."

Excerpt from Esther Huish's Diary

I have seen trees die, large hale trees green of leaf and limb whose roots, for no discernible reason, have simply perished and brought down with them the life they once nurtured. I suppose it was somewhere between Thomas's home and the Arcadia that Esther decided to die—or, more accurately, that she was through living. We did not speak on the return trip, and it was dark by the time we pulled up in front of the Arcadia. I helped Esther up to her room, and she collapsed on top of her bed.

That next week I stopped by her room as frequently as work permitted, but our vis-

its—as well as the visited—had deteriorated. Each day Esther dwindled some, as if
her life had sprung a leak that left her more
deflated with the dawning of every dusk. Esther no longer sat in her chair but lay inert in
her bed. Every night that week, after work, I
would come and sit in her chair, and sometimes there would be talk, but mostly there
was silence and melancholy. There were no
more walks, and I doubt that I could have
persuaded her to activity if I had had the
heart to. They were mean days, as spartan
of joy as they were in hope. Despair was not
monopolized by her. As the days passed, so
did my hope in Faye, and with each new day
of separation I became more insular, protecting myself beneath a sheath of anger.

It was late the next Friday night that I realized her locket was absent. I had worked
late, until ten, and came up to see her at the
end of my shift.

"Did your clasp break again on your
locket?" I asked softly.

"I removed it." I expected no explanation.
Her body rose with breath. "Would you get
me a glass of water?"

"Of course."

I went to the bathroom and returned with

her water. I had to lift her from the pillow as I guided the paper cup to her lips. She drank, then lay back. "Have you heard from Faye?"

"No. I can only hope that she's still just trying to sort things out. Though I'm beginning to fear that she already has."

"I imagine she is very busy," Esther said mercifully. There was a length of silence. "Do you suppose that in biblical times they named leper colonies?"

"I've never considered that. I suppose so. Why?"

"They give these homes names that make them sound like paradises. Arcadia, Elysian Hills, Green Pastures, Golden Living. They should name them after Western towns, like Last Stop or Death Valley. Places we go to die."

I gripped her hand, closing my eyes tightly. She continued speaking, her voice hoarse with grief. "There's no difference between this place and a leper colony. We gather all those with like affliction so they can die out of sight. Only, age is more frightening than leprosy. It's an affliction all must face." Her voice turned gruff. "Do not pity me. Pity yourself. The young are too afraid. They hold on so tightly to their lives that they squeeze the joy out of them." She closed her eyes and she was quiet, and I could hear her swallow. "Pity is a pathetic thing."

It was the last thing she said before she fell asleep.

I don't how late it was, but weeks later, when I was forced to recall the events of that evening, I calculated that it was probably past midnight when I finally left her room and descended the stairwell.

The Arcadia was dark and quiet except for the hum of a medicine refrigerator's belt and the hot breath of the heating ducts. As I came around the second-floor landing I heard a peculiar sound, a sharp yelp that sounded like an animal's cry. It came more than once and I followed the noise to Henri's room, slowly opening his door.

Inside, Alice stood above Henri's bed, crimson faced, her hand resting on his crutch. Henri was heavily panting between fierce coughs. I had not been alone with Alice since the night of the party, though we had of necessity passed each other in the course of our duties and she made no effort to veil her wrath. I attempted once to confront her about the night, but she made it clear that she would not allow it, so I settled in for the divorce of our association. Now I expected the worst of the encounter. Instead, she gazed at me with anxious, bright eyes.

"What are you doing?" I asked.

"Nothing."

I looked around the room but found no explanation for the sound I had followed.

"What was that noise?"

"What noise?"

"It sounded like a cry."

She laid the crutch back against the bed. "That was just Henri groaning. He wouldn't take his medicine." Just then Henri burst out in a fierce fit of uncontrolled coughing. Alice's voice turned meek, almost obsequious. "He sounds like he's getting worse. You seem to be the only one able to get him to take his cough medicine. What's your secret?"

"He doesn't always take it," I said.

Alice pulled the bed's covers up to the man's chin and stepped away from the bed. "We'll just have to pass on the cough medicine this time," she said congenially. She looked back at me. "I thought you had gone home."

"I was up visiting with Esther."

"She's fortunate to have a friend like you." She walked to the door and turned off the room's light. "See you Monday."

I wondered what was up.

chapter twenty

Ogden's Finest

"The winds of oppression that extinguish the flame of freedom in some only fan the fire of resistance in others."

Excerpt from Esther Huish's Diary

As I rarely worked on weekends, Saturdays and Sundays were especially lonesome, and I found myself searching for things to pass the days, not so much in absence of a companion as to keep my thoughts free of my companion's absence. Saturday morning I skipped breakfast, jogged five miles through snow-clad streets, then made my weekly excursion to the Laundromat, perusing *Esquire* as my laundry tumbled beneath a vibrating row of stacked quarters. After folding my clothes I returned home and had just settled in for college basketball when the doorbell rang.

I opened the door to a man not that much older than myself, stout and well built, wearing Levi's and a beige golf shirt beneath a ski parka. He wore a Cubs baseball cap, his eyes obscured beneath ebony-framed sunglasses.

"Michael Keddington?"

"Yes."

"I'm Detective Kinkaid of the Ogden Police Department. I would like to ask you some questions."

I looked at him quizzically. "Questions about what?"

"About Henri McCord."

I could not place the name. "I don't know who that is."

"You work at the Arcadia nursing home?"

"Yes, sir."

"You ought to know him," he said curtly. "He was one of your patients."

I suddenly realized who he was talking about. It had always just been "Henri."

"What do you mean, 'was one of my patients'?"

"That's what I'd like to question you about. May I come in?"

I stepped back from the doorway and motioned to the sofa. "Have a seat."

The detective entered the room and sat back into the sofa. He stowed his glasses in his coat pocket, then removed the coat as well.

"What do you know about Mr. McCord?"

"You mean personally?"

He nodded.

"Not much. He never talks. He's been really sick lately and hasn't responded well to the antibiotics."

"You take him his medications?"

"Not usually. I'm usually assigned to the third floor. But I do help out with him from time to time. Why are you asking?"

"Henri McCord died this morning."

I frowned. "I'm sorry to hear that. I saw him late last night. He was coughing pretty heavily. It didn't help that he wouldn't stop smoking."

"About what time was it that you last saw him?"

"Around midnight."

Kinkaid jotted something on a pad. "What else do you know about Mr. McCord?"

"Why would the police take an interest in his death? He was old. It just happens."

"Not like this," he replied cryptically. "What time did you leave last night?"

"Around midnight. I saw Henri on my way out."

He again scribbled in his pad, then stood. "That's all the questions I have for now. Thank you." At the door he asked, "You're not planning on leaving town, are you?"

"No. Why?"

"I'll probably be back in touch with you."

I went back to the game and by halftime had dismissed the visit.

Sunday was a repeat of Saturday's tedium. I stayed up late watching a black-and-white Hitchcock film, eventually falling asleep in front of the television. I woke late the next morning and was hurriedly dressing for work when the doorbell rang. Detective Kinkaid, the same man who had visited on Saturday, again stood in the doorway. This morning he wore a tie, a navy sports coat, and mirrored aviator sunglasses. A metallic blue patrol car was parked in the driveway with a uniformed police officer at the wheel.

"Mr. Keddington, I have a few more questions I need to ask you. I'd like for you to come down to the police station with me."

I glanced at my watch. "I can't now, I'm on my way into work."

He stared at me pensively. I felt suddenly tense. "If it's that important, ask me right now."

"I've already been in touch with your boss. She knows that you won't be in."

"What do you mean, I won't be in? What is going on here?"

Kinkaid spoke impassively. "Henri McCord died from complications of a severe beating. A witness has identified you as his assailant."

My heart froze. "Who told you that?"

He looked at me suspiciously. "Why is that of concern to you?"

I stammered, "Why wouldn't it be?"

He took a step backward. "Let's go."

I looked out to the driveway. "I'll take my own car."

"We'll take ours," he said assertively.

I had once before been in the backseat of a patrol car. It was as a child, when my father was arrested DUI and the police drove me home. I was anxious then, too.

The police station swarmed with the aftermath of the weekend and we passed a row of cubicles on the way to the interrogation room near the back of the building. A mirror flanked one wall and I wondered if a video camera was recording the proceedings from behind it.

Kinkaid stretched out his arms, then extracted from his pocket a card from which he read. "Mr. Keddington, you have the right to remain silent. Anything you say can and will be used against you in a court of law. You have the right to talk to a lawyer and have him present with you while you are being questioned. If you cannot afford to hire a lawyer, one will be appointed to represent you before any questioning, if you wish. You can decide at any time to exercise these rights and not answer any questions or make any statements. Do you understand each of these rights I have explained to you?"

"Are you arresting me?"

"This is just to avoid confusion in the case that you are arrested. Do you understand what I've just read to you?"

"In case I'm arrested?" I asked incredulously.

"Do you understand what I've just read to you?" he repeated.

I reluctantly nodded, and Kinkaid leaned

forward in his chair. "What do you know about the beating death of Henri McCord?"

"I don't know anything about it."

"You admitted to seeing Henri past midnight, yet you don't know anything about it?"

"No. It must have happened after I left."

He cocked his head. "And you didn't hear or see anything?"

I suddenly recalled my departure. "Actually, as I was leaving that night I heard a strange noise coming from Henri's room."

"What kind of noise?"

"Kind of a yelp. Like when you step on a dog's foot."

"Did you investigate?"

"I checked inside his room, but another orderly was already with him. She was just trying to give him his cough medicine. So I left."

He looked at me skeptically. ". . . Then you filed an incident report."

"There was no incident to report."

His countenance did not lighten. "Do you illegally use drugs, Mr. Keddington?"

"What does that have to do with anything?"

"It might have a lot."

"No, I don't."

"Do you sell or traffic drugs?"

I was indignant. "No."

Kinkaid leaned back in his chair; his demeanor changed to stone-faced sobriety. "Yesterday we searched your locker at the Arcadia Care Facility and found several stolen bottles of a controlled drug. Capsules from the bottles were found in the pocket of your smock."

I was shocked by the accusation and I felt my face flush. "I don't know how drugs could have gotten there."

"One of the orderlies tells us that there's been a problem with missing drugs."

"Who said that?"

"Why is that important?"

I was doing a better job of incriminating myself than the detective.

"Alice has control of all the medications in the Arcadia," I explained. "She's the only one with a key to the medicine locker." I suddenly understood. "Alice. It's Alice who is accusing me."

Kinkaid cocked his head as if considering his options, then opened his desk drawer and pulled out a form and began writing. After a minute he looked back up. "I am now placing you under a probable-cause arrest

for criminal homicide. I will take you downstairs in a few moments to book you into jail.
At that time you may make phone calls if you
so desire. Do you have any questions?"

My chest constricted. "How could you
think I did this?"

"There is sufficient evidence that you did."

"I need to speak with an attorney."

"You can call from downstairs after you
are booked into jail. Do you have a lawyer?"

"No."

"If you can't afford one, the judge will as-
sign a public defender to your case at your
arraignment."

"When is that?"

"Tomorrow morning. You may then contact
a bondsman and post bail."

"I'm spending the night in jail?"

He stood and took out a pair of handcuffs.
"That you are. Please stand and put your
hands behind your back."

"I can't believe this is happening."

"A few days in jail will make a believer out
of you."

To this day I wonder if there is a Jack Lord
course in one-liners at all police academies.

chapter twenty-one

The Nightmare

". . . even the most horrible of nightmares is laced with the promise of dawn."

Excerpt from Esther Huish's Diary

In the police station's basement, my fingers were rolled across a large inked glass plate and pressed against the requisite forms, handled as if they were not attached to the rest of my body. My clothes were swapped for the one-piece blue jumpsuit of a felon, and I was taken to a cage. In a brief snapshot of my predicament, when my mind was clear enough of panic to perceive my circumstance, I wondered what Faye would think to see me dressed down like this. Despairingly, I doubted that she would even care.

The next morning I was awoken at seven

o'clock and taken to the cafeteria for cold breakfast with the day's lineup of fresh inmates. We were given fifteen minutes to eat, then were shackled with waist chains and leg irons, and with the exception of a few of the more belligerent, our hands were cuffed in front; then the twenty-two of us were marched down through a tile underground passageway to a long wide corridor, to await arraignment. Opposite the hall from us, feeding into the same room, was a larger group of men likewise cuffed but clad in the bright orange jumpsuits of misdemeanants.

A rotund, ball-faced judge read my charges with clerklike efficiency. As I was standing accused of a felony, he automatically entered a plea of not guilty, then asked if I could afford legal representation. When I responded in the negative, an affidavit was given to me to list my personal property and financial assets, then a legal defender was assigned and I was given a roll-call date for the following Monday. My bail was set at seventy-five thousand dollars. It might as well have been for a million. I was allowed to call a bail bondsman, a terse Iranian man who refused my collateral for such a sizable bail, and I was taken back to the cell block. I had seen too many movies of people being arrested at lunch and bailed out before dinner. Maybe it's that way if you have friends on the outside.

The next six days passed in a horrifying blur. Monday I was brought again before a judge. This time there was a woman in the room standing near the judge's podium. She had fawnlike eyes and straight, dishwater blond hair. She wore a blue-and-gold silk scarf around her neck and a red wool business suit. She was thin, but her stomach protruded in evidence of pregnancy, when she was likely showing but not enough to safely assume. Her nose was red as if she had a cold, and I noticed a wadded handkerchief protruding from her coat pocket. I thought she looked too young to be an attorney.

When the judge had completed the requisite legalities, I was allowed to step aside to confer with my new advocate. She smiled as she reached out her hand in introduction.

"Hi, Michael, I'm Amanda. I've been assigned as your public defender."

It was the first time in days that I had spoken to someone who didn't seem to immediately hate or fear me. She reassuringly

touched my arm, then looked down to pe-
ruse my folder. "You're in a bit of trouble,
aren't you?"

"A world of it."

"Criminal homicide with an addendum of
drug possession thrown in for good measure."

I glanced around the room. "Can you get
me out of jail?"

"Have you tried to post bail?"

"I don't have enough collateral."

"I suppose we could try for a pretrial release. Tell me about your references."

"What do you mean?"

"The court wants some assurance that you
won't skip town. Do you have family locally?"

"No."

"How about friends?"

I was hard pressed to come up with a
name. "There's an elderly woman at the rest
home I worked at."

Amanda frowned, then looked again at
my folder. "Your record shows that you have
no previous criminal record. What did you
do before you started at the nursing
home?"

"I took care of my mother before she died
of cancer. Before that I went to college for a
year. I was an honor student. In fact, I was

just awarded the University of Utah's presidential scholarship."

"Congratulations," she said. I never would have thought to convey such sentiments under the present circumstances, and it made me painfully aware of the greatness of disparity between her and me. She could leave when she wanted to.

"If there is anything you can do to get me out of here, please do it."

She looked at me empathetically, biting her lower lip. "Presidential scholarship? We might have a chance for a pretrial." She turned away from me, caught up in sudden contemplation.

I spoke after her, "Excuse me. When will I see you again?"

She turned back. "Oh, sorry. I'll be back in touch later today."

Late that afternoon an officer came for me and I was released and given back my clothes. In all I had been incarcerated for eight days. I called for a cab and arrived home around seven. The milk I had left on the table had turned rancid, and I ended up skipping dinner and went straight to bed. Bed, but not sleep. Slumber was elusive, and when it came, offered small reprieve, my nightmares opting for equal time with my daytime's horrors. I dreamed that I was in a darkened, spacious parlor, the windows enclosed by black silk draperies and the room encompassed about by large, black-stemmed bouquets of ebony flowers. I was soon aware that I stood in a line of mourn-ers, strangers, all dressed in black, pro-gressing toward a casket upheld by a linen-shrouded bier containing Henri's bat-tered corpse. As I approached I suddenly recognized that it was not Henri inside, but my father's lifeless and disheveled body, a depleted bottle at his side. I turned away in revulsion, only to be grabbed by the corpse. Unable to free myself from its grasp, I was slowly dragged into the box and closed in under its lid.

I woke panting, fiercely struggling to free myself from beneath the layered covers of my bed.

The next morning at dawn's light I drove downtown to see Amanda. I arrived at the public defender's office before any of the at-torneys had, entered with the receptionist, and sat down, thumbing through *Popular*

Science magazines while the phone rang without cessation. A few minutes after nine Amanda walked in carrying a cinnamon roll and a capped Styrofoam cup. "Oh hi," she said to me. "Did we have an appointment?"

"I'm sorry. I just came down."

She tossed her head in the direction of her office. "Come on back."

Amanda's desk and office were cluttered with file folders and stacks of papers on official-looking stationery and a few specimens of local flora dying of malfeasance. There were two plastic trays of Girl Scout cookies on her desk. Her phone rang as we entered. She excused herself and took the call as I continued to survey the small, eclectically adorned room.

The wallpaper was white and tactile, like burlap. There were two framed academic degrees mounted above a large framed photo of Amanda dressed in corduroy hiking shorts, tank top, and hiking boots. She was sitting on the tailgate of a pickup truck with a golden retriever at her feet. A moment later she set the phone back in its cradle and lifted a folder with my name typed across it.

"Thank you for getting me out," I said.

"You were fortunate. The judge was in a good mood."

"You look really young. How long have you been a public defender?"

"It will be six months this March."

"How long have you been an attorney?"

"A little over seven."

My brow furrowed. "Have you ever represented a case like mine?"

"That depends on what you mean by a case like yours. I've never handled a caretaker abuse, but this isn't my first homicide."

"How many homicides have you handled?"

She hesitantly replied, "Three."

"Did you win any of those?" I asked flatly.

"Only one went to court. The other two plea-bargained."

"What about the one that went to court?"

"The jury found him guilty," she said reticently. I bowed my head into my hands.

"If it makes any difference, I graduated near the top of my class."

"How near?"

She gazed at me, dismayed at my skepticism. "Top twenty."

"I'm sorry. I was just hoping for someone

with a lot of experience with this kind of thing."

"I understand. I'm sure you are quite anxious." She set down the folder. "A few things that you should know. Anything we discuss is protected by attorney-client privilege, meaning I cannot discuss or disclose anything you tell me."

"So ask me if I'm guilty."

The phone rang again. "Just a minute." She confirmed a court date with a client, then hung up. "I never ask a client whether or not they committed a crime."

"Why not?"

"The jury does not find you innocent, they find you not guilty. They're not the same thing. The state has the burden to prove beyond a reasonable doubt that you are guilty. If you tell me that you did this—in fact, you enjoyed beating this man and are likely to do it again—it will be difficult to be real motivated to defend you."

"I didn't do it," I said.

She showed no reaction.

"So what do I expect now? What's the process?"

"In another week we go back to court for a

preliminary hearing, where a neutral magistrate determines if the state has sufficient cause to try you. If he does not dismiss your case, about a week after that you'll be bound over to a district judge, who will set a date for trial."

"And how long until that happens?"

"Usually ninety to a hundred and twenty days."

The phone interrupted us again and she smiled apologetically as she answered it. I couldn't decide if four months was a good or bad thing. I lifted from her desk an acrylic bauble paperweight that encased a scorpion and examined the creature. As she set down the phone it rang again almost immediately.

"How many cases are you working on right now?" I asked.

"As of today I have one hundred and six."

That night it started snowing again, falling in tandem with the day's sun. At ten o'clock the phone rang. It was a newspaper reporter for the *Ogden Herald Examiner.* It took me a moment to understand what she was saying. She was just checking her facts.

chapter twenty-two

The Aftermath

"When I consider the hardships that some others must face, my troubles seem foolish and petty—a succession of quixotic battles. To God, perhaps, they are all windmills."

Excerpt from Esther Huish's Diary

The article was diminutive—a one-column squib on page six of the *Herald Examiner*'s metro section—but for its consequence it might as well have been a banner spread across the front page of the *New York Times.*

LOCAL MAN CHARGED FOR BEATING DEATH
IN NURSING HOME

Michael Keddington, a 22-year-old Ogden man, was arrested for suspicion in the beating death of an elderly black man in the Arcadia Care Facility. . . .

There was one benefit to the article. For

the first time since my arrest, I was able to deduce the course of events that had transpired the night that Henri died. The sound I heard as I left Esther's room was undoubtedly Henri's cries as Alice beat him, probably with his own crutch. As the night progressed, Henri's bronchitis, exacerbated from the assault, had worsened until he lapsed into a coma and was rushed to the hospital accompanied by the responsible nurse on second-floor duty: Alice. When the doctors removed Henri's clothing they discovered the recent wounds, and fearful of discovery, Alice blamed them on me. Then, to bolster her claim, she planted drugs in my locker and informed on me again. Hell hath no fury like a woman scorned, quoth the saw. It wasn't until then that I understood that hell ran a distant second.

By 10 a.m. the first waves of the article's repercussion crashed down on my shore. The phone rang.

"Michael, this is Dean Scott from the university."

"Dr. Scott, it's good to hear from you."

He was uncomfortable with my greeting. "I'm afraid you won't think that when I have concluded."

"Is something wrong?"

"In light of recent developments it has become expedient that the university scholarship committee withdraw your scholarship."

The pronouncement stung. "Recent developments? You mean the newspaper article?"

"I mean the criminal charge."

"But I'm not guilty."

"To be perfectly candid, in the case of this scholarship, your guilt is almost irrelevant."

"How could that be?"

"Imagine the embarrassment it would be to this institution to bestow one of our most prestigious scholarships on a candidate charged as a felon."

I was dumbstruck. "Will the scholarship be reinstated when I am exonerated?"

The dean spoke hesitantly. "That presents a predicament. Scholarship bylaws dictate that in an unforeseen incident such as this, the board must immediately bestow the scholarship on the next available candidate."

"I am not guilty of this crime."

He was unsure of what to say. "You have my number. Call me when this is over and we'll talk."

"You won't be able to give me the scholarship, will you?"

There was hesitance in his voice. "We'll talk."

I was still reeling over the call two hours later when Amanda showed up on my doorstep carrying a leather portfolio over her shoulder.

"I didn't know attorneys made house calls."

"Believe me, it's not common," she said lightly. She brushed snow from her leather bag. "There have been some developments. May we talk?"

"I was just making ramen for lunch. Have you eaten?" I asked.

"No. Not yet. Maybe just something to drink."

She sat down at the kitchen table while I went to the refrigerator.

"I have Coke."

"Love one."

I brought the can to the table and set it next to a glass. She popped its tab.

"You wouldn't believe the calls I've been getting off that *Herald Examiner* piece," she said as she poured the drink. "It was fortunate that it was printed after your release. The judge never would have released you."

I set my bowl on the table. "That's reassuring," I said sarcastically. "How can the *Herald Examiner* print something like that? It's written as if I were already convicted. Isn't that slander?"

"Libel," she corrected. "And it's not. Once charges are filed, it's news." She punctuated the explanation by sipping her drink. "The media attention has put some real pressure on the state health department, and now they're calling in all their big guns. Heads are going to roll, and everyone is out to save their own."

"What is the health department's interest?"

"They are the body who accredited the Arcadia. Not only does this incident make them look bad but it opens them up to possible civil litigation. Of course, the Arcadia is also open to litigation if they can't walk away with a conviction." She poured the rest of the can into the glass. "To be frank, no one cares who is convicted as long as someone is and soon."

"What are my chances?"

Her brow furrowed. "If this goes to court, it's a roll of the dice at best. Despite what is preached about innocent until proven guilty, the truth is there's a presumption of guilt on the part of any jury. Do you understand that? They're thinking, If this guy didn't do it, then why is he here? Then there are the specifics of your case. The daughter of the head of Human Services implicates you—a relative newcomer to the home—of abuse, and since there are no other witnesses to the crime, it's her word against yours. From the standpoint of eight jurors, you have a credibility problem. Alice is the daughter of a prominent and popular government official involved in helping children and elderly at risk. Your father had a criminal record and died an alcoholic. Correspondingly, stolen drugs are found in your locker. Alice is an RN and has worked at the Arcadia, a facility with a previously sterling record, for nearly three years. You have only been at the facility for a few months when this occurs. To boot, you're a college dropout and, from what you've related to me, pretty much a loner. In addition, you're a man and she's a woman. In a case of abuse, that's not going to fall in your favor."

She looked at me with manifest concern. "Who do you think a jury will more likely believe?"

I felt like I had just been convicted. I turned

off the burner and sat down at the table, leaving the pan on the stove. "What do we do?"

Amanda took a deep breath. "That's why I'm here. There is another way through this. Like I said, the powers that be want a head. Any head will do, and they're willing to deal in order to get it. The prosecution has offered a plea bargain. If you will plead guilty to the lesser offense of criminal negligence—a class A misdemeanor—you will be given a two-week jail sentence, a week of which you have already served, a five-hundred-dollar fine, and in three years the conviction will be expunged from your record."

"And it appears in the newspaper that I pled guilty."

"I would expect it."

I buried my head in my hands. "What if I don't?"

Amanda leaned forward so there would be no mistaking the gravity of her words. "If convicted of this crime, you could face one to fifteen years in a federal penal institution, and the conviction would remain permanently on your record. You would forever be a convicted felon. In a case as public as this, I would not expect leniency from the judge."

I raked my hair back with my hand. "I can't believe we're having this conversation."

Amanda looked at me sympathetically. I leaned back in my chair, stretching my back. "What if I plead no contest?"

"The prosecution won't go for it. They need to transfer the blame from the institution to an individual. They need a guilty plea. They need a goat."

"And I'm their goat," I said despondently. Amanda sipped her drink.

"If I decide to fight this, how will you approach it?"

She looked concerned by my question. "I haven't had time to consider strategy yet. Do you have any strong character witnesses?"

"How about the Arcadia's director, Helen Staples? Helen doesn't even like Alice."

"It's not Alice who's being charged. And you would be asking her to indirectly testify against the daughter of the head of Human Services. You can bet Starley Richards has already been in contact with her, as well as all her superiors the entire Christmas tree up. She was pretty tight lipped when I spoke to her this morning."

"Helen was?"

Amanda nodded, and it pained my heart. I

thought Helen was above such things. I considered her a friend.

Amanda pushed her chair back and re-
crossed her legs. "I'm sorry, Michael. I know
it's a tough decision. There is nothing fair
about any of this. But in your best interest I
have to recommend that you plead guilty."
She looked down at her watch, then stood.
"I'm sorry, I've got to get to court. You have a
week to make your decision." She took a final drink as she stood, draining the glass.
"Just consider your dilemma carefully before
you decide."

I couldn't imagine that the day could get
worse, as the snow piled as high and as re-
lentlessly as my troubles. Around seven the
phone rang.

"Hello."

There was a moment of awkward silence
before a disgruntled voice boomed from the
receiver. "Is this Michael Keddington?"

"Yes it is."

"This is Dr. Murrow. I wanted to inform you
that I have facsimiled the article from this
morning's newspaper to Faye and I spent a
good deal of time with her on the telephone.
She has assured me that she wants nothing

more to do with you. I am not going to warn
you again. Just stay away from her. I have
friends in local government, and if you continue to harass Faye, I will see to it that it is
reflected in your term of incarceration."

I hung up the phone. It was an idle threat,
I told myself, but it was not the threat that
had left me aching. For the first time since
her departure, Faye's abandonment had
been confirmed.

To be a man, I believed, is to be stoic—to
wear one's pain behind an impenetrable
mask of granite and withstand the assaults
of life on one's feet. But it is one thing to bat-
ten down the hatches against turbulent seas
and quite another to be flung naked into the
tempest.

I have heard it said that courageous men,
soldiers of great strength, cry out for their
mothers when mortally wounded. It would
be a shameful thing for a man to say he
wanted his mother, but in searing honesty,
that is what I wanted: an omniscient, compassionate being to shelter me up in her
arms—to speak words of reassurance and
love. Perhaps this is when I understood
what it was about Esther that I had connected to and embraced—that she had, in

some way, fulfilled my mother's absence. I had been warned to stay a thousand yards away from the Arcadia; it had been stipulated as a point of my release; but at that moment it was just paper. I put on my coat and drove to see Esther.

Alice was at work at the front counter as I entered the foyer. She looked up at me, her countenance initially expressing fear, then evolving to coolness.

"What are you doing here?" she asked acerbically.

"What do you think you're doing?"

"Patient logs."

I glared at her vehemently, though she appeared unfazed.

"You shouldn't be talking to me, Michael," she said cavalierly.

"You shouldn't be talking to anyone. Do you realize I could go to prison because of your lies?"

A hateful smile crossed her face. "Well, I'm sure you'll have no problem finding a girlfriend in there."

I had never before had such loathsome thoughts; wisely I had kept them bridled by the reality of my perilous circumstances.

"This is going to come back on you," I warned.

"What will?" she asked innocently.

"What you did to Henri."

She looked back down at her work and her voice softened. "Do you really think anyone will believe you? You'll only look like a scared boy trying to save his own neck."

I leaned over the counter toward her, and she suddenly appeared frightened. "Just keep your damn mouth shut." I glared at her as I stepped into the elevator. I was still very much agitated from the confrontation as I opened Esther's door.

"Esther?"

From the darkness came a weary voice, lilted with disbelief. "Is that you, Michael?"

"It's me."

"Let me touch you," she said softly.

I went to the side of her bed and took her hand.

"I heard that they put you in jail."

"They did."

"What is happening?"

"I have been accused of beating Henri to death."

"Where did they get that idea?"

"Alice told them. That Friday when I left

your room I heard a noise coming from Henri's room. I walked in on Alice. She was standing by his bed, holding his crutch. I didn't know it then, but she had been beating him. When Henri was rushed to the hospital a few hours later, she blamed it on me."

"I warned you about her."

"You did." I rubbed her smooth hand. "I could end up in prison for the next fifteen years."

"What are you going to do?"

"I don't know. I've been offered a plea bargain. If I plead guilty, I can get off with just a few weeks in jail."

"Plead guilty to something you didn't do?"

"Sell my birthright for a get-out-of-jail-free card." I raked my hair back. "I've already lost, Esther. I've lost my job. The university took away my scholarship. But what hurts the most . . ." I was suddenly speechless, overcome by the pain of Faye's desertion. Esther rubbed my hand.

"You haven't heard from Faye?"

"Her father called to say that she has assured him that she has no more interest in our relationship."

"And you believe him?"

"What can I think?" I said in exasperation. "I haven't heard from her since she left."

"It is a difficult time for her too. But Faye wouldn't abandon you."

I breathed in deeply. "I just don't know."

Just then Helen opened the door. In the darkness it took her a moment to perceive my form.

"What are you doing here, Michael?"

It was a stupid question, I thought. "Visiting Esther."

"You were given a restraining order. You are not to be within a thousand yards of this facility. You're not even to make a phone call here."

"Good heavens, Helen, this is Michael," Esther said ardently. "He is not a criminal."

"That isn't for me or you to decide. You must leave, Michael, or I will have to call the police."

Esther squeezed my hand. "Have faith, Michael."

I rose from her side and Helen stepped back from the door as I left the room. As I started up my car I thought that I would have liked to ask Esther what exactly I was to have faith in.

chapter twenty-three

A Second
Visit

"There are more lines today in the looking glass. Time is the warden of all flesh."

Excerpt from Esther Huish's Diary

I find that it is easier to procrastinate making difficult or unpleasant choices until time or circumstance forces the decision by default. I had waited the full week allotted to call Amanda, even though I suppose that I knew what I would do the moment my options were presented. Fear had presented a compelling case, while higher ideals of truth and justice hightailed for cover. The shadow of the unknown was too thick. There was too much that could go wrong. Too much uncertainty. One thing, however, grew less obscure. I learned who my friends were, or, in most cases, weren't. Perhaps, most obviously, Helen's position was clearly manifest. She was just like everyone else, scurrying like a cockroach to avoid a brogan. I didn't blame her for wanting to save her neck, as I would have condemned myself in the same verdict. But I didn't have to like it.

The last person I expected to hear from that week was Helen. There was a strange divinity to the timing of her phone call. It came the day before I was to give the prosecution my decision.

"Michael, this is Helen."

I did not respond.

"I know you don't want to talk to me, but you need to hear this."

"What do you want?"

"Esther is dying."

My chest constricted. "Right now?"

"No. It is still gradual."

"Esther's been dying ever since I took her to see Thomas."

"It's beyond that. The day before you came, Esther bumped her leg against something. Not hard, but enough to cut it. Gangrene has set in. She needs surgery before it spreads, but she won't submit to it."

"What kind of surgery?"

"A femoral bypass. But her leg is already

gangrenous. If it doesn't work, they'll have to take her leg."

"How long will it take to spread?"

"It could take months, but it spreads further each day."

"Why don't you do something about it?" I said hostilely.

"I've tried, but she's still angry at me for making you leave. You're the only one she will listen to." She paused preparatorily to her proposal. "If you can come tonight I will make sure that no one knows you're here."

I thought of the possible implications were I to be caught—even, for a moment, considered if it were some kind of a trap—but just as quickly derailed my paranoia for Esther. "What time?"

"Ten-thirty."

"I'll meet you around by your office."

"Thank you, Michael."

"Save it. I'm not doing this for you."

Beneath the veil of nightfall, Helen escorted me in through her office door. She had carefully assigned each orderly a task that would take them out of our way, and at her insistence I did not remove my hooded parka until I reached the darkness of Esther's room.

It was obvious that Helen was being cautious for herself, not me, and as soon as I was with Esther she left the floor to avoid implicating herself with my presence.

"Esther?"

The form under the comforter stirred slightly.

"Esther, it's me. Michael."

"Michael?" the voice rasped. "Does Helen know that you're here?"

I sat down on the bed next to her, taking her hand. She lifted her head from her pillow.

"Helen tells me that you've cut your leg."

She was silent for a moment. "Oh, that."

"She says that you need to have your leg operated on."

Esther said nothing.

"The gangrene will spread. It will kill you."

Her voice sounded weary and resigned. "It is only inevitable."

"There is nothing inevitable about gangrene."

"There is nothing so inevitable as death," she replied.

I sat there in the darkness without response, frustrated at her indifference for her own life. "You can't do this," I said brusquely. "You can't just give up on life."

There was suddenly matching ardor to her voice. "You plan to forsake your name and your love by pleading guilty to a crime that you did not commit, and you tell me that I must not give up on life? We're two of a kind, Michael. All that death requires of us is to forsake the future." Her voice dropped an octave. "At least I waited more than forty years." At length Esther sighed. "You were right, you know. Maybe life gives us second chances, or maybe it doesn't. But it doesn't really matter. We'd probably just make the same mistake again." She lay back in her pillow and turned her face away. There were no words, no inspiration, to save either of our lives. There was nothing to do but go away.

Helen stopped me as I unlocked the door to my car.

"Did you have any luck?" she asked somberly.

I opened the car door. "If you wanted luck, you came to the wrong man."

chapter twenty-four

The Womb

"Tonight I took a stroll under the stars with Thomas. He spoke profoundly of trivial things which, I suppose, is better than the inverse. Under the moon's glow he somehow looked different to me. Perhaps it is, has always been, that the moon gives visage only to that which is already within us."

Excerpt from Esther Huish's Diary

Beneath a brooding moon, I fled the Arcadia, driving west through silent neighborhoods until the cast-iron street lamps became more sparse and the streets grew more dim, leaving my destination, the winter-cloaked grounds of the city cemetery, illuminated only by what the heavens bequeathed.

The graveyard was still. Its large iron gates had been padlocked since dusk and the second-story lights of the sexton's home glowed amber behind drawn drapes. I parked my car at the cemetery's west end, near my mother's grave. The street was as deserted as the grounds. The yard was fenced off just a foot past the sidewalk by a five-foot wrought iron spear fence separated every ten yards by red-stone, cement-capped pylons. I scaled one of the pillars and dropped down into the pristine, crusted snow. The snow was as high as three feet in places, and I plodded through it toward my mother's grave, beneath the oak and willow canopy that shadowed the outer perimeter of the yard. My mother was not buried far from the fence—resting beneath a small granite marker. Plastic flowers still remained at its base, buried to their necks in the snow. I stood before her stone.

Caitlin Keddington
A Loving Mother
August 1, 1944–October 30, 1988

I brushed back the snow from the monument.

What do I do, Mother? I thought. *What do I do?*

I knelt before the grave, clutching the stone with my gloved hands. Then I suddenly screamed out the words: "What do I do?" My breath hung frozen before me in the chill air while my voice echoed back from the frozen landscape, mocking me with my own uncertainty.

Perhaps it was Esther's haunting accusation of my spiritual suicide that still resonated across my thoughts, or maybe it was the cold name staring back at me from the granite headstone. Whatever the spark, something happened that, to this day, I cannot explain and can only partially describe. A feeling came over me. A feeling I remembered from childhood. One night, as a small boy, I woke crying from a nightmare. My mother rescued me and as I sat in her lap, whimpering and gazing fearfully into the dark, tormented by the unseen terrors it held, my mother gently rocked me, repeating with sweet assurance, "Don't you cry, little man. There's nothing in it but your own fears." In her arms I knew I was safe. Somehow, that same peace had suddenly enveloped me, and I felt as serene as if again in my mother's embrace.

And then the insight came. I was suddenly confident of what it was that I must do. I did not know the consequence that lay at the end of the appointed path, simply which path it was to be. It was a push that should have left me terrified. But it didn't. For the first time in my life I saw things differently. For the first time things were clear.

There were things about my mother I had never understood. Such as why she had kept my father's name. I had assumed that, like most of the unpleasantnesses of her life, it was something that she had done for me. To spare me any embarrassment that it might engender. But there was something else about my mother that was even more peculiar.

She wept when she learned of my father's death.

It was suddenly clear to me why. My mother had kept his name because she had never stopped loving him. As inconceivable as that seemed to me, there was something about him that was still worthy of her love and she not only seemed to love him after he abandoned us but she loved him more so.

At that moment I understood that Esther had been right, not just about me but about my father as well. That my father never loved alcohol. It owned him, but he did not love it. But he did, perhaps, love us. In his sober moments he would sometimes weep bitterly for the pain he caused my mother and me. I remembered something that I rarely allowed to enter my mind, lest I allow mercy to enter with it and plead in his behalf. Just before my father left us, he came to me and begged me for my forgiveness—an appeal I responded to with hatred and rejection. I remember his face as he left. It was twisted in anguish, but not condemnation. He understood, he said; he deserved no less. And then he was gone.

Esther was right. My father had never stopped loving us. But he knew from years of failure that he couldn't free himself from the chains of his addiction, so he sacrificed his own heart to set us free. He died alone.

For the first time in my life I wept not for the pain my father had caused us but the pain of his life. I wept for him. And in some mystical, miraculous way, in those tears I found something that had eluded me since I was old enough to understand its absence from my life. I found peace. As elusive as it had seemed, it had been where it had always been, concealed behind a door of forgiveness.

I looked again at the name on the grave and I was certain of what forgiveness required of me. To set aside the known shackles of the past for the untested wings of the future. I was to protect and honor my father's name.

chapter twenty-five

The Plea

"It is my observation that too often this world builds monuments to those it stoned in the flesh."

Excerpt from Esther Huish's Diary

The office fell quiet, and Amanda, poised over an earthen cup of hot coffee, stared at me in stunned bewilderment, as if she had misunderstood. "No plea bargain?"

"No."

She sat back in her chair, studying me. "Do I need to remind you of the seriousness of these charges?"

I shook my head. "I know things don't look good for me. I won't pretend that I'm not afraid. But I can't do it. I can't convict myself of this crime. Even if it means going to prison for my innocence."

She leaned back in her chair. "A judge will

likely interpret your attitude as lack of re-
morse."

"I can't do it, Amanda," I said softly. "I can't
forsake my name. It is all that I have left."

She steepled her hands under her chin.
"When did you decide this?"

"Last night, at my mother's grave."

She sighed. "I admire your courage,
Michael. Unfortunately, most of my heroes
are martyrs."

"I have no desire to join either rank. I just
have to do what I have to do. Where now?" I
asked.

"I'll call the prosecution and tell them
we're going to trial." She stood up. "Then you
and I have a lot of work ahead of us."

Amanda Epperson was a transplant from
Woodstock, Illinois, a picturesque suburb of
Chicago that is sometimes used by film pro-
ducers for feature backdrops. She had met
her husband, Phil, while completing her
undergraduate degree at Northwestern University, and he dutifully followed her to the
University of Utah Law School, where he
worked as a driver for UPS and wore a
brown uniform.

Amanda was already pregnant when she

passed the bar and was expecting a girl in mid-May. In the games our minds devise to torture ourselves, I conceived that according to a jury's whim I would see Amanda's child either as an infant or likely not until she was a teenager.

Amanda wore hiking boots whenever possible, drove a Jeep Wrangler with a detachable tan canvas top and a bumper sticker that read, *When the sun's out, I go topless.* She loved the outdoors, vacationed each year in Zion National Park, and I suspect that she came to Utah as much for the mountains as the quality of the law program.

In the months leading up to my trial, I met with Amanda three or four times each week to work on my case. She was bigger and I imagine more uncomfortable each time I saw her. I became accustomed to her radical cravings, and perhaps my greatest contribution to the case, outside of my recollection of my visit to the veterans hospital with Henri, was my discovery of the best after-hours outlets for a pint of Snelgrove's burnt almond fudge ice cream or yogurt-covered pretzels.

Out of financial desperation, I took a day job as a convenience store clerk on the north side of Ogden and in deference to both of our schedules, Amanda and I usually met after work, oftentimes after Phil had gone to bed. It became obvious to me that my case had become a personal crusade for Amanda, and I was sure this was due, in no small part, to her becoming convinced of my innocence. Such things are not supposed to affect a legal defender, but only an automaton could be that detached. Such creative causes must be dictated by passion, and without passion we are doomed to mediocrity. We can't help it, we're just wired that way. I was fortunate that Phil was about as tolerant as a husband could be, and more than once he brought home Chinese or Italian for the three of us as we reviewed testimony in their apartment. I confess that there were times I found it difficult watching such a loving couple, in light of Faye's absence. I learned later that he did ask her once if she was becoming too emotionally involved with me, and she kissed him and said no and he left it at that. He is a good man and I'm convinced he will be a good father to their child.

The weeks passed in a succession of highs and lows, a countdown to perhaps a much larger one. It was probably not unlike the emotional swings of a political candidate as election day nears. Except I was hoping not to serve any term. For better or worse, the anxiousness of the cause had the anesthetic effect of pushing my other concerns to the more shadowed corners of my mind, and there were days that I nearly forgot the two women who had all but consumed it the months before. The night before my trial, one of them called.

chapter twenty-six

The Trial

"There are times that I have been tempted to protect my heart from further disappointment with cynicism. . . . But it would be like poisoning oneself to avoid being murdered."

Excerpt from Esther Huish's Diary

The restraining order provided a two-way mirror of sorts, enabling Esther to look into my life while I could not look back at hers. I had not spoken with Esther in quite some time and I did not recognize her voice at first. It had changed, fallen even more slow and tired than when last we spoke. It worried me.

"Michael."

"Is that you, Esther?"

"Do you go to the court tomorrow?"

"Tomorrow morning."

"I won't be able to come," she said sorrowfully.

"How are you feeling?"

She did not answer my question. "Did
Faye come?"

I did not want to answer, more for her than
myself. "No."

There was a pause of considerable dura-
tion and I could hear her irregular breathing.

"I never told you how proud I am of you for
standing up to this. You are courageous."

"You were right, Esther. I just hope fate is
kind."

"You are a good boy. God will be merciful."

"I hope you're right. Thank you, Esther."

Her voice began to falter. "Come see me
when it's over."

"I will if I can."

She hung up the phone and I wondered if
I would ever see her again.

Amanda arrived at my house a full hour before the trial, as I was just finishing getting
dressed. The night before I had asked her
how I should dress for the day. "Guileless as
a Sunday school altar boy," she replied.

I wore taupe slacks with a white, long-
sleeved oxford shirt, a necktie, and a tweed
jacket that I had borrowed from Phil.

Amanda and I had been up late the night
before reviewing testimony and rehearsing

likely questions the prosecutor would pose to the witnesses and what those answers might be. I suspect she did this more for my sake than hers, as I would have gone crazy without her company. She expected the trial to last for two or three days.

I climbed into her Jeep.

"How'd you sleep?" she asked.

"Very little."

"I expected as much."

"And you?"

She smiled. "I can sleep through anything. Even this baby." She glanced over at me. "I had a thought last night. I think the prosecution will call you to the stand."

"I thought you said that they couldn't."

"I said that you don't have to testify against yourself. But in a trial as emotionally charged as this one they might call you up as an adverse witness, expecting you to plead the fifth. To the jury it will look like you're hiding something."

"What do I do?"

"I think you should testify. You'll do all right. In any case it will likely do less harm than refusing to take the stand." She grinned and set her hand on my knee. "Don't worry about it. They may not call you up; it's just a hunch. I want you to remember, no matter what happens today, to stay calm. This is just the first day, and it's the prosecution's show. It's almost all going to be negative. There's nothing the prosecution would like better than to fluster you into looking guilty at the get-go." She spoke seriously but with a confidence I had not previously detected—her trial face, perhaps, but a mask of confidence all the same, and it set me at peace. She took my hand. "I think we have a strong case. Believe in that."

Her optimism did not prepare me for what we were to encounter as we arrived downtown. The hedged walk and grounds surrounding the courthouse were rife with humanity, teeming with newspaper, television, and radio reporters, senior citizens, advocacy groups for the elderly, and just people who needed someone to hate. A small girl held out a handwritten placard that read simply, *Leviticus 20:9.* I wondered what the scripture said.

Like most of my peers, I had arrogantly supposed that I belonged to a more civilized generation than our fathers', but what I saw that day changed my paradigm. Yesterday's lynch mobs are alive and well, in spirit if not in action, fed from the same trough of prejudicial indignation. Amanda held my arm as she hurried me past the throng as if she were embarrassed for the gathering and hoped I hadn't noticed it.

I had never before been in trouble with the law or set foot in its courts, so my expectations were culled from years of Saturday matinees starring Gregory Peck or Spencer Tracy and a steady diet of *Perry Mason* reruns. The courtroom was larger than I had anticipated, though still not large enough to accommodate the incensed public that thronged to my gallows. The room was high ceilinged and elliptically shaped and brightly lit with hanging deco glass light fixtures. The room's benches were highly varnished yellow oak, as were the jury box, the court reporter's well, the judge's bench, and the ledges that connected them. The judge's chair was flanked by a large navy blue flag bearing the beehive insignia of the state of Utah.

I counted more than a dozen journalists in the room scribbling on the long narrow pads of reporters. Every seat in the gallery was taken, and the back of the room was lined

shoulder to shoulder with the standing, leaning against the paneled oak wall.

Alice sat behind the bar, near the prosecution's desk. Next to her sat a large, well-
dressed man whom I recognized as her father,
Starley Richards. I had seen Richards on the
six o'clock news, talking to reporters about my
impending trial, his voice and gesticulation rising in swells of righteous indignation for the
waywardness of today's youth, and I wondered
when was the last time he and Alice had had a
heart-to-heart. The jury was already seated,
and at the bailiff's pronouncement the room
rose as the judge entered. The judge, the Hon-
orable Howard Wells, was a short, tonsured
man with a gleaming scalp and a gruff face. He
had that rare panache that allowed a trial to
proceed unencumbered by his personality
without allowing any doubt that we were in his
room.

Following the formalities of the court, the
trial began.

The prosecutor began the trial with an
emotionally charged appeal in which he
graphically described the horror of my al-
leged crime. From the winces on the jurors'
faces I believe he effectively made his point.
It was the first time I had actually seen the

prosecutor, and up to this point he had been only a caricature—a title slapped on some hated adversarial force no less in my mind than an agent of evil. He was a thin man with sandy red hair and small wire-framed glasses. He wore a suit too large for his body, and it was not a far stretch to imagine him standing against the dugout fence as the other kids got picked first to play. I would be the first to admit that in another place and time, I probably would have liked the man. Confronting our adversaries is always an epiphanous experience.

Amanda's opening statement was a well-stated counterpoint. She agreed with the prosecution that abuse by a caretaker was a heinous crime, certainly as heinous as child abuse, and that in the case of Henri McCord, it was exceptionally horrible. She then reminded the jury that what was on trial was not the horror of this crime, as that was a given, but the guilt of a young man in committing it. A young man with no previous history of criminal wrongdoing, assault, or even a speeding ticket. A young man who was not only an excellent employee at the facility but an honor student who was recently awarded the University of Utah's prestigious presidential scholarship and a son who lovingly took care of his mother as she died of cancer.

"Indignation, righteous or otherwise, is a weapon. We must be cautious in its handling," she said, "for a weapon will kill the innocent just as dead as the guilty."

At the conclusion of her remarks the prosecution began to present their case against me, calling up a line of subpoenaed nurses and emergency room personnel who had attended to Henri at his death. They were followed by an expert witness, a doctor who had clearly been well rehearsed in his testimony. Their intent was to establish in the jurors' minds that Henri's death was caused by the beating and not a natural result of endless weeks of chronic asthmatic bronchitis. They displayed grisly color photographs of Henri's wounds, rendered all the more macabre by being attached to a corpse with an amputated limb. As the human body ages, the thin layer of fat tissue beneath the skin diminishes, rendering it far more susceptible to damage. A simple bump against a bed rail that would not leave a mark on a child may result in a massive bruise on a senior. The force of Alice's blows was sufficient to tear skin.

The trial took a one-hour recess for lunch, and we ate at a cafeteria inside the facility to avoid the crowds that beset us both—as the mob had started in on Amanda as well. The afternoon testimony varied little from the morning's, and the congregation of onlookers sufficiently heated the room that the judge ordered the doors open to allow air circulation. The day's testimony ended unspectacularly, with one surprise—one of the prosecution's witnesses, a doctor, stunned the prosecution by stating that he doubted that the extent of the beating would have killed a man without severe bronchitis. The prosecution abruptly finished with the witness and Amanda jumped on the chance to further establish the premise in the jurors' minds. Amanda had cross-examined each of the day's witnesses, but not with great intensity, often speaking from behind our table, as our defense strategy did not hinge on whether the beating had caused the death as much as it did on my guilt for the action, though she still endeavored to cast doubt in the jurors' minds as to whether Henri would have survived the week even without such an assault.

At the end of the day Amanda and I

stopped for aspirin and tacos before she dropped me off at home. At her advice I kept the television off, made myself some tea, set the alarm, and crashed.

Amanda picked me up at seven the next morning, and this time we parked in the underground garage reserved for courtroom personnel, avoiding the throng that, enticed by the night's press coverage, had grown still larger than the day before. The day's proceedings began with the prosecution calling up another medical professional, better screened and rehearsed than their last, who basically reiterated the previous day's summations. Then the prosecutor again asserted the points they felt they had established. I began to understand their strategy, that repetition breeds consensus, and if you repeat the same accusations enough times, people will simply start believing them along with a host of other unproven recriminations.

The prosecutor called Detective Kinkaid as the next witness. Kinkaid sauntered up to the witness box, slumping cavalierly in the chair. He wore a polyester jacket with a neatly pressed shirt and a knit tie.

"Detective, what is your position with the Ogden Police Department?"

"I am a homicide detective."

"How long have you been employed in that role?"

"I was transferred to homicide about three years ago. But I have been with the force about eight."

"You are assigned this case involving Henri McCord, is that correct?"

"Yes, sir."

"Please tell us the events that you were involved with in the early hours of January seventh."

He rubbed his mouth with his hand. "Dispatch received a call from McKay-Davis Hospital that an elderly man had been severely beaten and was in cardiac arrest."

"Did you go to the hospital and investigate?"

"Yes, sir."

"What did you find?"

"I found that Mr. McCord had been repeatedly bludgeoned. Marks indicated that he had been struck at least sixteen times."

"Did you garner a statement from anyone at the hospital at that time?"

"I spoke to the doctors." He pointed. "Dr. Williams there. And a couple others."

"Did they corroborate that Mr. McCord had been assaulted?"

"Of course. It was obvious. Look at the pictures."

The prosecutor nodded. "Was there a representative from the Arcadia nursing home present at that time?"

"Yes. Miss Richards had brought him."

"How was she acting?"

"She seemed real shaken up by the ordeal."

"What did she say to you?"

"She said that she had not known that he had been beaten until it was pointed out by the doctors. I asked her if she had any idea about who might have done this, and she said that she had seen Mr. Keddington coming out of McCord's room around midnight, a couple hours after his shift had ended. She said she thought it strange because he was not assigned to the second-floor patients. She also said that he had acted strangely, had kind of a deer-in-the-headlights look about him."

I shook my head incredulously. Amanda

put her hand on my knee to remind me to remain calm.

"In the course of your investigation did you interview Mr. Keddington?"

"On several occasions."

"Did anything unusual transpire in those interviews?"

"He initially denied knowing who Henri McCord was, but when I pressed him he claimed to suddenly remember."

"Did he deny being with Mr. McCord the night of the assault?"

"No. In fact he told me that he was there, but he didn't see anything."

"When he learned of Henri's death, how did he respond?"

"Initially he said that he was sorry . . ."

"Sorry?" the prosecutor interjected. "Sorry for what?"

"I assumed that he was just sorry that he died, I guess."

The prosecutor maundered toward the jurors.

"When did Mr. Keddington learn that he was accused of assaulting Mr. McCord?"

"The morning that I brought him into the station."

"What was his response at that time?"

"He wanted to know who had accused him."

"What else happened that morning?"

Kinkaid looked at the prosecutor blankly. He had forgotten this part of the rehearsal. The prosecutor prompted him. "Before you picked up Mr. Keddington, did you visit the Arcadia?"

"Oh, right," he said. "Yes, I did."

"For what purpose?"

"We had been told by a witness"—he glanced at Alice—"Miss Richards, that she had seen Mr. Keddington stealing drugs and she believed that they were still in his locker."

"Did you find drugs in his locker?"

"Yes we did. Three bottles of Percocet. We also found individual capsules in his smock."

"How did Mr. Keddington respond to that information . . . about the drugs?"

"He denied that he used drugs."

"After you drove Mr. Keddington to the station, did you interrogate him?"

"Yes, I did."

"Did he say anything unusual in the interrogation?"

"He wanted to know who had accused him of stealing drugs."

"What did you say?"

"I asked him why that was important to him. He seemed real interested in who had turned him in."

"When did you decide to arrest him?"

"When he figured out that it was Miss Richards. For her safety, I thought that I had better incarcerate him."

The prosecutor stepped away. "Thank you, Detective."

"Thank you, sir."

"Cross?" the judge asked.

Amanda looked up. "Yes, Your Honor."

She approached the officer.

"Outside of Miss Richards's testimony, did you interview anyone else at the Arcadia?"

"Yes, ma'am."

"Did any of them accuse Michael as well?"

"No."

"Did any of them suspect Michael?"

"No."

"Did anyone else see Michael leaving Henri McCord's room?"

"No."

"Did anyone else at the Arcadia suspect Michael of stealing or using drugs?"

"Not to my knowledge."

"The warrant you received to search Michael's locker was based solely on the testimony of Miss Richards?"

"Yes."

"So you are telling us that the whole of your suspicion is based solely on the testimony of one person, Alice Richards?"

"Yes, well, that and my interviews with Keddington."

"Do you suspect that, based on the witness's testimony, you were biased toward Mr. Keddington before you interviewed him?"

"It would be kind of hard not to be."

"You have made it sound as if Michael Keddington acted suspiciously in wanting to know who had accused him. If you were falsely accused of a crime, would you personally have any interest in who had accused you?"

"I object, Your Honor," the prosecutor said. "The witness's hypothetical actions in this regard are irrelevant."

"Sustained."

"Your Honor, I am attempting to establish

that my client's actions are not unusual and certainly not grounds for suspicion."

"Move on, Counselor."

Amanda looked flustered. "Of course you would," she said to Kinkaid.

The prosecutor threw his hands up dramatically. "Your Honor . . ."

"That will be enough of that, Counselor," the judge said forcefully. "Strike Mrs. Epperson's remark from the record."

"I apologize, Your Honor," she said contritely. She turned back to Kincaid. "When you found the drugs in Mr. Keddington's smock, did you look in there yourself, or did someone else suggest that you look there?"

Kinkaid looked stumped. "I don't remember, ma'am."

Amanda stepped away. "No further questions."

The prosecution conferred among themselves for a moment, then as Amanda had predicted I was called to the stand. As I sat down I looked over the gallery, and from the vantage of the witness box, I saw something that I did not expect. At first I did not believe what I saw. Six rows back, near the center of the gallery, sat Faye. I had not seen her right off, as she was sandwiched between two large men and looked exceptionally small. Her hair was styled differently, and as I looked closely to verify that it was she, we shared eye contact. Her eyes were not distant and she reached up and touched her lips, and despite everything I had heard, or hadn't, I knew somehow that she was with me. Just her being there was proof of that, and it gave me strength.

The prosecutor approached me, his chin raised in a confident air.

"Mr. Keddington, do you know Alice Richards?"

I looked over at Alice, who sat listlessly, gazing on the proceedings with dispassionate eyes. "Yes. I worked with her."

"What else do you know about Alice?"

"She's the woman who accused me of beating Henri."

"When did you know that it was she who had testified against you to the police?"

"When I was arrested. The police officer told me that it was she."

"When you were released from jail, did you go to see Alice?"

I glanced over at Amanda, who looked dismayed by the question.

"No. I went to the Arcadia to see a friend, and Alice was there."

"Did you speak to her?"

"Yes."

"Did you tell her, and I quote, she should not be speaking to anyone and should just keep her damn mouth shut?"

Amanda looked mortified. At the time it had seemed natural and inconsequential, and I suddenly thought that I probably should have told her about the incident.

"Yes, I did."

There was an audible gasp from the gallery.

"Do you realize that that exchange constitutes witness tampering, a third-degree felony?"

"I just lost my temper," I said stupidly.

"You lost your temper," the prosecutor repeated, as if he liked the remark. "That's not a good excuse for breaking the law, Mr. Keddington. The same way you lost your temper the day you struck Henri McCord?"

"I object, Your Honor," Amanda said, rising. "It has not been established that my client struck Henri McCord."

"Sustained, Counselor."

"I'll rephrase the question. Did you lose your temper and strike Henri McCord?"

"I have never struck any of the patients in the Arcadia. I couldn't do that."

"Do you use drugs, Mr. Keddington?"

"No, sir. I have never used drugs before."

"How do you explain the three bottles of Percocet that were found in your locker at the Arcadia as well as the pills in the pocket of your smock?"

"They were not put there by me."

"Then how did they get there?"

"I don't know. Alice was in charge of the prescriptions."

"Are you saying that Alice Richards put them there?"

"I really can't say."

The prosecutor nodded his head, then turned and took a few steps toward the jury box as if he had just proven some point vital to his case. "Your father was an alcoholic, was he not?"

Amanda quickly rose. "I object, Your Honor. The witness's father's actions are not relevant to this inquiry."

The prosecutor smiled confidently. "Your Honor, it has been demonstrated that the cycle of physical abuse is an act that is often perpetrated and carried down in families. As this is a case involving severe physical abuse, I find it very relevant."

The judge said, "I will allow it, only so far as to establish some reasonable act of familial abuse."

"Thank you, Your Honor." He turned back to me. "Your father was an alcoholic?"

"Yes."

"So, there was alcohol in the home."

"Sometimes."

"He drank every day?"

"Yes."

"And there was only alcohol sometimes."

"My mother didn't allow it in the home. She would dump it out or hide it when he fell asleep. So my father only brought in the bottle he was drinking."

"Did your father ever beat you?"

"No."

"Did he ever beat your mother?"

"No."

"He never beat your mother when she poured out his alcohol?"

"I saw him push my mother up against a wall once."

"And that was it?"

"He stopped when he saw me. He wasn't a violent man."

The prosecutor rubbed his chin. "I don't know if I find it more disturbing, or revealing, that you confess that your father threw your mother against a wall, but he was not a violent man. What is your definition of violent?"

"I would consider that act violent," I stammered. "What I meant was, not usually. He was more likely to fall asleep or cry when he drank."

"Is it possible that your father beat your mother outside of your view?"

Amanda interjected. "I object, Your Honor. How could the witness answer that question?"

"Withdraw your question, Counselor."

"How did your mother act after a night of your father being home drunk?"

"Hurt. She was a good woman. She didn't deserve to be treated like that. No one deserves to be treated like that."

"She would be ashamed to learn of these proceedings, would she not?"

"She would be afraid. She spent much of her life afraid. But she would have nothing to be ashamed of."

He smiled cynically. "In the past two years you have dropped out of school and left a job under pressure of being fired. The Arcadia was the first job you have been able to hold in some time, that is, before you were given a restraining order, was it not?"

"Yes, but that's because I was taking care of my mother."

"That's all, Mr. Keddington." The prosecutor turned to Amanda. "Your witness, Counselor."

"The defense does not wish to cross-examine at this time, Your Honor."

"You may be seated," the judge said to me. I rose from the box and returned to my seat. I looked up at Faye once before I sat down, then glanced toward the jury box. Not a single juror looked toward me. Somewhere I had heard that that was a bad sign.

The prosecution resumed. "I would like to call to the stand Miss Alice Richards."

Alice rose and walked to the front of the room. She avoided eye contact with me, only glancing at me briefly.

"Miss Richards, how long have you worked at the Arcadia Care Facility?"

"It will be three years this July."

"During that time, were there ever any reported incidents of patient abuse?"

"Not to my knowledge, no."

"You were at work on the night of January sixth?"

"Yes."

"Please tell the jury what happened that night."

"I was working the night shift. A few hours into my shift, I went in to check on Henri. He had been on our watch list because he had acute bronchitis and wasn't improving. When I came into his room, he was comatose."

"You are sufficiently qualified to make that assessment? I mean, you knew that he wasn't just asleep?"

"I am an RN, so I have medical training. Henri didn't look right. His breathing was so shallow that it was almost imperceptible. I felt his forehead and it was very hot."

"What did you do then?"

"I called the paramedics and they rushed him to the hospital."

"At that time did you suspect that any abuse had taken place?"

"No. He had been very sick for several months."

"When did you learn that Henri had been beaten?"

"When the ER doctors removed his shirt. He had severe bruises all over his body." She pointed at the previous exhibit. "Like those pictures. It looked to me like he had been repeatedly struck by something. In fact, some of the wounds were still bleeding."

"What was your first thought?"

"I didn't know what to think. Then I remembered hearing a strange noise and seeing Michael come out of his room. I thought it peculiar because Michael's shift ended several hours earlier."

"Did you tell the attendant medical personnel that you suspected him?"

"Yes, I did."

"Then what happened?"

"Henri went into cardiac arrest. He died right after that."

"Are you aware that Mr. Keddington has accused you of abusing Henri?"

"Yes."

"What do you have to say to that?"

"I think Michael is afraid."

"I object, Your Honor. Conjecture on the part of the witness is irrelevant."

"Sustained. Strike the witness's remark from the record."

The prosecutor continued. "Is it true that

Mr. Keddington entered your nursing home on the night of January twentieth—roughly ten days after he was released from his responsibilities?"

"Yes, he did."

"What was the purpose of his visit?"

"I don't know."

"Did you see him enter the Arcadia?"

"Yes. He came straight to me."

"Did he speak to you?"

"Yes."

"What exactly did he say?"

"He told me not to talk to anybody. Then he told me to keep my damn mouth shut."

"Did he threaten you?"

"From someone who had beaten an elderly man, I took that as a threat."

The prosecutor stepped back and looked toward the jury and nodded his head as if to punctuate the remark. He slowly turned back toward Alice. "There were pills found in Mr. Keddington's locker. Do you know what they were?"

"They were bottles of Percocet that belonged to some of the patients. Percocet is a painkiller."

"What were they doing in Mr. Keddington's locker?"

"I could only speculate. They belonged to the patients."

"Are you in charge of prescriptions at the Arcadia?"

"Yes."

"Were you aware that those pills were missing?"

"Not those specifically. There are so many medications that I'm not always good about throwing out old pills. Though I did notice recently that things seemed to be disappearing, and on several occasions I had to reorder some prescriptions."

"Do you remember about when it was that these medications started to mysteriously vanish?"

"Around the beginning of November."

"And what was significant about that time?"

"It was around the time Michael came to work at the Arcadia."

The prosecutor paused again for emphasis, and I looked up at the jury, and two of the jurors quickly looked away.

"Did you suspect Mr. Keddington of stealing the drugs?"

She turned and looked at me. "No. I thought he was a decent guy."

"Did you suspect him of physical abuse?"

"No. I didn't. He acted decent enough. In fact, some of the residents are his friends."

"Do you consider Michael Keddington capable of abusing a patient?"

"Objection, Your Honor. This calls for conjecture."

"Your Honor, we are seeking to validate the character of a fellow employee, as a character witness conjecture is relevant."

The judge did not answer immediately. "I'll allow it."

"Again, Miss Richards. Do you consider Michael Keddington capable of abusing a patient?"

She furtively glanced at me. "I don't know. I think he has had a rough time in life and needs some help."

"No further questions, Miss Richards." He stepped back to his seat and looked once at the jury, then the judge. "Your Honor, the prosecution rests."

The judge surveyed the room. "Would the defense care to cross-examine the witness?"

Amanda rose. "Not at this time, Your Honor."

The judge glanced up to the courtroom clock, then reiterated his warning from the previous day. "It is nearly five o'clock. I adjourn this trial until tomorrow morning. I counsel the jurors to not watch television news or read anything concerning this trial and to avoid forming any opinions until we have heard from the defense. You are not to speak to anyone concerning this trial, including witnesses and legal counsel. If you are approached by someone who wishes to speak to you concerning this trial, you are required to report that individual to this court." He pounded his gavel. "This court now stands adjourned until tomorrow morning at nine o'clock."

chapter twenty-seven

A Last Good-bye

"There are those whose primary ambition in life is to leave their names chiseled on some small corner of this globe. But this is folly. The greatest tragedy is not to die unknown by strangers, but unloved by our companions."

Excerpt from Esther Huish's Diary

At the judge's adjournment, the noise in the courtroom rose in an excited cacophony. I turned around to look for Faye. She was making her way against the exiting crowd toward me. Her countenance was grave and she looked wan. She stepped in front of me and we looked at each other like strangers, unsure of each other's hearts. I could then see that her eyes were moist, and she came close and lifted her arms around me. I held her tightly. Just then a woman in silver bifocals and tall permed hair reminiscent of a beehive walked up next to me, her face contorted with hatred. "I hope you rot in hell for what you've done."

I could feel Faye tense and she moved to turn back toward the woman, but I held her. "Let her go, Faye."

Her jaw clenched. "How can you do that?"

"It won't help me."

She fell back into me, burying her face into my shoulder. Amanda turned and said to me, "Michael, I need to talk to you." She looked at the woman pressed against me. "Is this Faye?"

Faye looked up, then instinctively glanced down at Amanda's stomach. "I'm Faye."

She held out her hand. "I'm glad you came," Amanda said. "You two would probably like to be together."

Faye looked at me. "My parents don't know I'm here."

"There's room at my place," I said.

Amanda touched my arm. "Let's get out of here. We can cover tomorrow's agenda on the way home."

The three of us stopped for dinner at a Japanese restaurant, and it seemed that Amanda did most of the talking as Faye retreated slightly into herself. My stomach hurt and I drank a bowl of miso soup. Amanda dropped us off at the house around eight and I let Faye in, and she flung a leather-bottomed backpack from her shoulder and fell back into the couch. "Let's talk," she said.

I sat down across from her, my fingers pensively knit together. Faye sighed.

"I am sorry that I have left you alone through all this. I have been so confused. My father told me about taking you to dinner. He thought you were past tense to me, so he felt free to tell me about his threat ... I'm sorry, Michael. I was so hurt when I left. But you thought you were protecting me." She paused. "I decided to wait a month ... just to clear out my head. But it became clearer every day how much I love you and want you ..." Her forehead wrinkled with anxiety. "Then all this happened. My father faxed the article to me, then told me that you had confessed to beating the old man to death."

I was suddenly angry, as much at Faye as her father. "And you believed him?"

She began to tear up. "No, I didn't."

The room fell quiet, and Faye came over and sat down next to me. She put her arms around my neck, then gently pulled me into her, maternally pressing my head into her breast. We lay there silently and I could hear Faye's heart pounding. Finally Faye spoke.

"Amanda made it sound like this might end tomorrow."

"It could. I come home free, or will not see this place for years. Maybe you too."

She pulled back to look into my face. "No, Michael. I won't desert you again."

Her promise did not raise my spirits. "What if I'm found guilty?"

"I will stay with you as long as they let me. I don't know if they'll just take you away or what . . . We'll see, I guess. I won't desert you, Michael," she repeated.

"What if I'm found not guilty?"

She thought about it. "I'll fly back to school. I have an exam Monday, but it's spring break the week after next. And we'll spend every minute of it together."

I sighed. "I can't believe that this time tomorrow night I could be in prison."

Faye's eyes moistened. "Ask for a commitment, Michael. Let me prove my love to you. Please, give me the chance."

I looked at her and my eyes also moistened, but I would not do it. It would be like exacting a deathbed promise. It would not be right. So I just lay back into her, and she pulled me tightly against her again and kissed me; then she just held me lovingly, and it was the best thing I have ever felt. A half hour later, just before eleven, the phone rang. I debated answering it, then deciding it might be Amanda, lifted the receiver. A feeble voice came from the receiver.

"Michael."

It was Esther. I was surprised at the deterioration of her speech since the day before.

"Did Faye come?" she asked. The words came driven and desperate, as if she were unable to stop them. Still, they were tinged with reticence and fear for the answer.

"She's here with me now."

There was silence on the other end, and I could imagine her praying in gratitude. "I knew she would."

"Are you all right?"

Her voice was soft. "I'm just so tired, Michael. I'm not doing too well. You'll come see me when this is over?"

"First thing."

"Michael." She paused for the longest time until I wondered if she had perhaps fallen off to sleep. ". . . I wanted to tell you that I love you."

As trite as those words may seem, I am still astonished at their power from the right mouths and at the right times. "I love you too, Esther."

I could hear the receiver fumble around in its cradle before it went dead.

chapter twenty-eight

Esther's Letter

"Oftentimes the difference between a lynch mob and a square dance is a good fiddler."

Excerpt from Esther Huish's Diary

Utah's climate is as diverse as its landscape, from the perennially baked red-rock tabernacles of southern Utah to the snow-capped mountains to the north, where March enters like a lion and is just as likely to go out as one. That night the snow came again, and although I hoped that the inclement weather might lessen the crowds at the trial, the night's media again added to the assembly, and were tickets sold to such events, I would have expected scalpers out in the storm, hawking the better seats. I suspect that they smelled blood.

The night with Faye had, in some ways,

left me more fearful of the day, as it was a powerful reminder of just how vacant I felt without her, and I knew it was possible that a verdict could be handed down by late afternoon, forcing our separation.

"There are going to be a few surprises today," Amanda said nebulously as the three of us drove to the courthouse.

"What kind of surprises?"

She seemed suddenly grave. "There's a few that for the time being I would prefer to remain such. One you need to know about is that I am going to call you up first to testify. I want you to tell the jury what happened that night. About the sound you heard and about finding Alice in the room. But let me caution you. Whatever you do, don't make it sound like you're accusing Alice. We can't prove Alice did anything, and the prosecution would have a heyday vilifying you. I just want to plant seeds of doubt. I will also ask you if you beat Henri McCord."

"You think it will make a difference?"

"I want the jury to hear it from you. You're a very genuine and sincere man. I would like to have them see that before I call my other witnesses. I think it will especially appeal to a couple of the mothers in the jury."

Faye took my hand.

"Do you think the prosecution will cross-examine me?"

"Hard to say. Probably not, if we don't give them anything they can actually dispute. They've already hit you with their best shot, and they don't want to end with something less potent. If you don't make any accusations that we can't stand behind, they should pass."

"You mean accusing Alice."

"Exactly." Her countenance lightened. "Nervous?"

"I think I'm digesting my stomach lining."

"I think it will be a good day," she said casually, as if she had forgotten that my next fifteen years depended upon it.

About a half hour into the morning's proceedings, I was called back into the witness box. The bailiff reminded me that I was still under oath, then Amanda approached, waddling maternally, and I wondered if it was exaggerated for the jury. She wore a maternity blouse and stretch pants that highlighted her condition, and after watching her in action for two days, I did not think it a coincidence. Amanda left little to chance, and I now thought it fortunate that she was pregnant, as she had clearly aligned herself with me and no one wants to see a pregnant woman lose.

"Good morning, Michael," she said with the pleasant tonality of a neighbor's greeting. I instinctively smiled, which I suspect she had hoped for.

"Did you like working at the Arcadia Care Facility?"

"It took a little while to get used to some of it, but once I knew the people, it was a great job."

"On the night of January sixth, the night of Henri McCord's beating, you had clocked out at nine o'clock, but you did not leave work until after midnight. Why were you there so late?"

"A friend of mine—one of the residents—wasn't doing too well. She had taken to bed and I was hoping that I could cheer her up."

"What time did you leave?"

"I don't know the exact time, but I arrived home around twelve-thirty, so it was probably a little after midnight."

"What floor were you on with your friend?"

"I was on the third floor."

"As you were leaving that night, did anything unusual happen?"

"I heard a strange noise coming from the second floor. I stopped to investigate and found that it was coming from Henri's room. But when I checked, all I found was Alice standing next to his bed."

"What was she doing?"

"Just standing there. She said she was trying to give him his medicine."

"Was she holding his medicine?"

"No. She had one hand on his crutch. I assumed that she had given up trying to get him to take it."

"What kind of noise did you hear?"

"It was a kind of yelp. My first thought was that there was an animal on the floor."

She paused as if she herself were considering the revelation for the first time.

"Michael, did you like Henri McCord?"

"I didn't know him well. But I suspected that he was lonely, being so old and the only black man in the home. I felt sorry for him. I suppose I liked him."

"Michael, did you beat Henri McCord?"

"No, ma'am. I was hired to take care of him."

Amanda stared at me with kindness. "Thank you, Michael. That is all, Your Honor."

Before she could return, the prosecutor

stood. He looked excited, as if he had suddenly stumbled upon something.

"Mr. Keddington, what is your disposition toward blacks?"

"My disposition is favorable."

"Have you ever participated in an anti–affirmative-action demonstration?"

"No, sir."

"Do you dislike blacks?"

"Of course not," I said curtly. "That would be like disliking elderly people because they are old."

Amanda smiled and the prosecutor turned away, frustrated that the trail led nowhere. "That's all."

"You may be seated, Mr. Keddington," the judge said.

Amanda winked at me as I stepped from the box and she stood.

"The defense would like to call to the stand Ms. Helen Staples."

This was one of Amanda's surprises, as I considered Helen a more likely witness for the prosecution than us. Helen walked up to the witness stand. She wore her smock from the nursing home.

"Ms. Staples, what is your position at the Arcadia Care Facility?"

"I am the director of the facility."

"How long have you been employed in that position?"

"Nearly eight years."

"You are the one responsible for hiring Michael Keddington, is that correct?"

She looked at me. "Yes I am."

"What kind of an employee was Michael Keddington?"

"He was a very conscientious one. He worked hard."

"In your opinion, would Michael have beaten a patient?"

"No, he would not."

"You sound relatively certain of that."

"I watch my employees very carefully, usually when they don't know that they are being watched. I have seen how he treats the patients. He treats them with dignity. It's something you either have or don't. A person who would beat a patient would not be very likely to spend his off hours at the facility visiting them."

Amanda moved toward the middle of the floor. "Your Honor, Ms. Staples has brought with her today a letter from one of the Arcadia's residents, which I would like to read in Michael's behalf."

The prosecutor stood. "I object, Your Honor. This is not relevant character evidence."

"Your Honor," Amanda countered, "this letter constitutes grounds of pertinent character trait."

"Overruled."

The prosecutor persisted. "Your Honor, this letter is inadmissible on grounds of hearsay."

"The defense cites hearsay exception rule eight-o-four as the declarant is physically unable to attend court," Amanda said.

"Why is this witness unavailable, Counselor?"

Amanda was suddenly hesitant, and as she looked back at me, I felt the uneasiness of her gaze.

"The woman who wrote this letter died early this morning."

The words took my breath away. I gaped at Amanda, then glanced over to Helen, who looked on dolefully as if to affirm Amanda's statement. My eyes watered and I dropped my head in my hands, then moved them over my eyes. The judge patiently observed the interaction, then said, "Hearsay objection overruled."

Amanda opened the letter. "This letter is

dated March twenty-fourth. Three days ago."
She cleared her throat.

Dear Jurors,
My name is Esther Huish. I have spent the last seven years as a resident of the Arcadia Care Facility. I have been, by my own preference, alone for most of that time. That is, until last fall, when I met Michael Keddington. Despite my obstinance, Michael's acts of kindness eventually opened my heart to him. He would often visit me after work and he would keep me company. He is loved not just by me but also by all the residents that know him. I have collected their signatures of support in his behalf.

Michael has been accused of beating a fellow resident, Henri McCord. We hope for the speedy and severe prosecution of the person guilty of this great evil—for hurting one of our fellows. But we are certain that it was not Michael who committed this atrocity and fear that the true culprit might be allowed free. The harsh life Michael has lived has softened his spirit, not calloused it. Any society that destroys such spirits must reap what it deserves—bitter, angry sons resigned to a world that is as merciless as it is unjust.

If my son had grown to be a man, I would hope he would have been like Michael.
Sincerely,
M. Esther Huish

We, the undersigned, stand in support of Michael Keddington.

Amanda held the letter toward the jury.

"There are twenty-eight signatures here. I would like this letter displayed as exhibit M."

The prosecutor said loudly, "I object, Your Honor. These signatures are from senior citizens. These folks are puerile; they don't know what they are signing."

"Your Honor, every signature was collected from the legally competent and notarized by Ms. Staples," Amanda countered. "And I am dismayed by the prosecution's attempt to prejudice the jury by declaring all senior citizens as puerile."

The judge was likewise annoyed by the prosecutor's remark. "You are overruled, Counselor."

"These are all the questions I have for Ms. Staples."

Amanda sat down. She leaned over toward me. "I'm sorry, Michael. I couldn't tell you before you testified."

I sat there quietly, then brushed my cheek. She reached over and took my hand. I put my other hand on top of hers. I was unable to speak.

Across from us the prosecution consulted with one another.

"Would the prosecution like to cross-examine the witness?" the judge asked impatiently.

The prosecutor looked up, still humbled by the last reprimand. "We would, Your Honor." He rose slowly, pausing briefly at his desk to finalize his rebuke. Helen warily watched him approach.

"Ms. Staples, in the course of your eight years at the Arcadia, has your facility ever been charged with the abuse of a patient?"

"No."

"Until now, that is," he corrected. "Imagine, eight years with a spotless record, and within two months of Michael Keddington's employment, there is an incident. Don't you find that an unlikely coincidence?"

"I find it an unfortunate one."

"Did you ever suspect Mr. Keddington of substance abuse?"

"I would not have hired him if I had."

"When you were told that he had been found in possession of drugs, what did you think?"

"I was skeptical."

"Why skeptical?"

"Michael did not seem to be the type."

"So, you can accurately tell what type of person abuses drugs?" he asked facetiously.

"Often."

"Did Michael ever come into work under the influence of alcohol?"

"Not to my knowledge. I would have insisted he leave had I recognized it."

"Did he have a drinking problem?"

"Not to my knowledge. I have never smelled alcohol on him."

"And you would recognize it if you did?"

"Absolutely. My mother was an alcoholic."

He stopped the line of questioning, switching quickly to avoid the appearance of defeat. "Are you aware that as condition of his release from jail, Michael was given a restraining order from your facility?"

"Yes."

"That means he cannot have any contact with the home, by phone or in person."

"That is correct."

"Has he come into the home?"

She hesitated. "Yes."

"We have established that he entered your facility a few days after he was released from jail and spoke with Miss Richards, which you did not report."

"No. I asked him to leave, which he did."

"Did he come in again after that?"

Helen again hesitated. "Yes."

"When?"

"Eight weeks ago he came to see a resident at my request."

"Knowing full well that his presence was in violation of a restraining order, you allowed him into your facility?"

"I believed that it was a matter of life and death. The resident would not consent to medical procedures to save her life. I was hoping that Michael could get her to consent to medical treatment."

"Did he succeed?"

She looked at me and her face was sad. She said softly, "No."

"That is all," he said as he walked back to his chair.

"You may sit down, ma'am," the judge said.

Amanda stood. "The defense would like to call to the stand Dr. Raymond Heath of Ogden's veterans hospital."

The doctor, dressed in an oxford shirt and knit tie, walked forward and sat down. Amanda again stood.

"Dr. Heath, according to hospital records you examined Henri McCord approximately six weeks before his death."

"Yes, I did."

"According to the rest home's driving log, it was Michael Keddington who accompanied Henri McCord to your hospital." She pointed to me. "Do you recognize this man?"

He looked at me. "I remember speaking with him."

"For what reason was Henri McCord sent to see you?"

"Henri McCord was suffering from acute bronchitis. He was on some fairly high doses of antibiotics, but he was not recovering."

"What type of examination did you give Henri McCord?"

"It was a typical examination. I visually checked his sinuses, then listened to his heart and lungs."

"Did he remove his shirt for the examination?"

"Yes. I had him dressed in a gown."

"Did you find anything unusual during that examination?"

"I did. I found numerous abrasions on his body."

"What kind of abrasions?"

"Bruises all over his body. At the time I had thought that the man had fallen as he only had one crutch. I recommended that he get a wheelchair."

"Based on the scabbing and bruising, is it possible to determine when these wounds were inflicted?"

"It is possible to determine when trauma occurred by charting bruise progression."

"In the instance of Henri McCord, when would you say those injuries took place?"

"I estimate nine to ten days prior to his visit."

Amanda turned toward the jurors. "The jury should note that according to the Arcadia's employment records, Michael Keddington began working on November ninth, just four days before this visit." She looked back at the doctor. "You believe that these wounds were inflicted a full week before Michael came to work at the Arcadia?"

"It is actually not just my opinion; wound progression has a factually chartable progression. There is no chance that those injuries occurred less than five days prior."

"Did you point out these injuries to Mr. Keddington?"

"Yes, I did."

"What was his reaction?"

"He seemed concerned. He asked if they were bedsores."

"Were they bedsores?"

"No. They were clearly caused by a blow of some sort."

"To your recollection, did Michael Keddington say anything else?"

"He asked if I wanted his director to call the hospital."

"Is this consistent action with someone who has caused abuse, to call it to the attention of a superior?"

"Your Honor, this calls for conjecture; this man is not an expert."

"Overruled," the judge said. "Please continue."

"No, it is not consistent. Usually someone involved with abuse has already made up an

alibi for the injury. A fall. Walked into a door.
I've heard them all. Someone once told me
that aliens abducted their father."

His reply evoked a chuckle from the
gallery. Amanda looked content.

"Thank you, Doctor, that is all."

"Would the prosecution care to cross-
examine the witness?"

"We would, Your Honor." The prosecutor
approached the doctor confidently, swagger-
ing like a gunslinger.

"Doctor Heath, how long ago was it that
you examined Henri McCord?"

"It was in mid-November. About four
months ago."

"How many patients have you examined
since that time?"

"I would have to check hospital records."

"I don't need exact numbers. Best guess."

The doctor placed a finger to his forehead. "Maybe fifteen hundred. At least that
many."

"You have quite a memory, then, to remember one patient."

"Actually, I have an excellent memory. But
a one-legged black man is not quickly forgotten, either."

There was another laugh from the gallery.

"Do you remember what day of the week it was when you examined Henri?"

"No, I don't."

"But after examining fifteen hundred other patients, you can remember the exact stage his abrasions were in?"

"No, I couldn't remember that."

The prosecutor lifted his hands demonstratively. "Yet you have just testified to this court that you are certain that the bruises were caused nine to ten days previously."

The doctor was unruffled. "I know that because I checked the patient's records and photographs before I came to testify. Working with Medicaid requires that we take pictures of such things." He pointed to the exhibit. "They're not that far off from these, except they were not as recent."

The prosecutor stepped away from the stand. "I have no more questions."

Amanda fumbled through her portfolio, then rose. "I would like to call Alice Richards back to the stand."

Alice's father rubbed his daughter's shoulder in support. She stood and approached the bench. She gazed impudently at Amanda.

"Miss Richards, do you have a locker in the Arcadia?"

"Every employee does."

"Is there a combination lock or some means of securing that locker?"

"No."

"Do any of the lockers have locks?"

"No. They're made of wood. They're more like cupboards."

"So, it would be a relatively simple thing for someone to have placed those drugs in Michael's locker?"

"If someone had reason to, I suppose so."

"I'm glad you said that," Amanda said, repeating the words. "If someone had reason to. Is it correct that outside of Helen Staples, you are the only one authorized at the Arcadia to order prescriptions?"

"That is one of my responsibilities."

Amanda nodded at the confirmation, then walked back to our table and lifted a typewritten sheet of paper. "I am going to read to you a list of names. Leah Marsh. Anna Crockett. Doris Curtis. Lucille Haymond. Wilma Bettilyon. Harvey Stromberg. Clara George. Jakob Romney. Do you know any of these names?"

"Some of them were patients."

"Actually, they all were patients of the Arcadia," Amanda said. "Do you recall what they all have in common?"

"They're old," Alice replied flippantly. There was a respondent chuckle in the gallery, and Alice smiled at her own witticism.

"They all used Percocet—a highly addictive painkiller that is often abused," Amanda said. "The very drug that was found in Michael's locker."

Alice looked uneasy. "There is no way I could recall all the drugs the patients use."

"There is something else these people all have in common. Do you have any idea what that might be?"

"Your Honor," the prosecutor shouted from his chair, "the defense is badgering the witness. Miss Richards has already answered this question."

"I will answer the question myself, Your Honor." Amanda turned toward the jury box. "These people whose names I have just read are all dead. In fact one of them, Lucille Haymond, passed away more than a year ago."

"Like I said, I don't really remember them."

"Perhaps you can answer this. Why would you refill Lucille Haymond's prescription every month for the last year?"

Alice turned ashen. "I didn't."

"Actually, Alice, you did. For Lucille Haymond and for the other seven deceased residents' names that I just read. We have it in your own writing, corroborated by the pharmacy. Moreover, the pills that were found in Michael's locker were ordered, by you, for Lucille Haymond just two hours before Henri McCord died, and were not delivered until Sunday morning." She smiled serenely and her voice intensified. "There was no way Michael could have placed those pills in his own locker." Amanda stepped closer to Alice. "The pharmacist's receipt of delivery was signed by you personally. No one, except you, knew of them." She leaned forward, staring into Alice's face. "Did you place those pills in Michael's locker?"

Alice cowered beneath her gaze, then glanced over to her father as if searching for someone to tell her what to say.

"Alice, can you answer my question?"

"I want to speak with my attorney."

"The prosecution is not your attorney." Amanda pressed. "Answer the question, Miss Richards."

She still did not speak. The judge intervened. "Miss Richards, if what you are about to say is self-incriminating, we need to appoint counsel to represent you."

She burst into tears and began shaking her head. Amanda advanced like a boxer with an opponent in the ropes. "Alice, would you like to recant your story about Michael Keddington striking Henri McCord?"

"I don't have anything to say. I would like counsel."

Amanda held the moment until the only sounds in the courtroom were Alice's sobs, then she said softly, "The defense rests, Your Honor."

There was a moment of silence before the prosecutor rose for his closing statement, as the room was still spinning from the recent revelations. Amanda's presentation had been brilliant, and I should have been reveling in my new chances, but the joy had been equally matched by sorrow, and in hearing of Esther's death I felt as if a portion of punishment had already been meted out. No matter the outcome, I had lost something dear.

chapter twenty-nine

Closing Arguments

"A man came to the inn today seeking a room. There was a coldness to his mien which left me chill. I bore false witness in telling him that there were no vacancies. There is a reason that there are people whom we instinctively distrust. That which we endeavor to conceal from the world is revealed in our countenances."

Excerpt from Esther Huish's Diary

The prosecutor's closing argument was little more than a litany of his previous assertions, most of which now stood on trembling ground. He only briefly mentioned anything having to do with Alice's testimony. He spoke haltingly, stammering, and despite the circumstances, it was satisfying seeing the man scratch and his cocksure strut reduced to a grovel. The jurors watched him dispassionately, and I suspect that he ended his statement sooner than he had intended to avoid alienating them further. Contrarily, Amanda confidently approached the jurors, her face as bright as if she planned to invite them all over afterward to a backyard barbe-cue. Her hands rested strategically on the back of her hips as if to relieve the back pains of pregnancy, and I am certain that more than one of the jurors watched her sympathetically. She individually eyed each member of the jury.

"The prosecution would have you believe that Michael mercilessly beat an old man. Not just beat him, but beat him to death. They say that this young man committed murder. This young man who has never been accused of any sort of crime, was an honor student his first year in college, was awarded one of the university's most presti-gious scholarships, quit his job and school-ing to take care of his ailing mother, and is loved by the residents of the nursing home he came to work at. Can you really believe this charge?"

Without losing contact with the jury she pointed toward the courtroom doors. "But there are people outside who believe it. There are people out there screaming for justice who have no idea who Michael is or what happened the night Henri McCord was beaten. In fact, if any of your names were mistakenly printed in the newspaper instead of Michael's, they would be calling for you. You know that's true." Amanda looked toward the outer doors, though she might as well have looked around the room.

"The truth is, the prosecution has attempted to blur your vision with the emotion of this heinous crime, so as to falsely accuse a young man of committing it. The prosecution needs a scapegoat because they—and the public—demand it. The Arcadia needs a scapegoat because they are financially liable for what happened under their roof." She demurely advanced toward the jury and said, in a softer voice, "And deep inside, each of us wants a scapegoat because we don't want to believe that we're the kind of people who would let such villainy go unpunished. We're wired that way. So maybe we don't care quite so much who gets punished, as long as somebody does. That is why people are falsely charged of crimes every day in this country.

"It was the state's responsibility to prove that Michael Keddington beat Henri McCord to death. What did they actually prove? That Michael was outraged when he was falsely accused. Wouldn't you be? They proved that Michael's father was an alcoholic. Michael's not. Michael has suffered enough for that heritage; he should be congratulated for rising above that hardship, not condemned for it. He does not live life like a victim, nor does he ask for sympathy. Just a fair shake.

"But no matter how you feel about any of this, you must put all prejudice and passion aside and look at this one crucial fact. You have endured hours, too many hours, of witnesses talking about a crime being committed. No one disputes that. But amongst all those witnesses and expert testimonies, there was *only one person* who actually accused Michael of this crime, and she was the woman whose records show she should have been in Henri's room about the time these beatings took place. Then, upon cross-examination, this witness would not stand by her previous testimony. Then she pled the fifth when asked if she planted drugs in Michael's locker." Amanda's voice rose in climax. "Drugs that we can prove she illegally ordered. Drugs that were impossible for Michael to have put in his locker as he was nowhere near the facility between the time they were delivered and the time they were discovered in his locker. We know this. We can document it. And not surprisingly, it was this same woman who told the police where they could find those drugs. So, as the prosecution asked Michael yesterday, if he didn't put those drugs in that locker, then who did? I don't need to answer that for any of you. Black-and-white, the prosecution has no case. They have no evidence that Michael committed this crime. They have no motive for him committing this crime, and most of all, they have no witness.

"Does the prosecution really believe that Michael is a murderer? If they did, would they have offered Michael Keddington the plea bargain that they did? Plead guilty, they told him, and you will only spend a few days in prison. Is that how you treat someone who has savagely murdered an infirm elderly man? Now turn that around. If Michael were the kind of man who had committed this heinous crime, why wouldn't he jump for that offer? I would have. I would have because I know that juries may make bad choices when they become more involved in the emotion of a trial than in the truth of it. In fact, as his attorney, before I had the chance to examine his case, I advised him to take that plea bargain.

"You, we, are here because Michael

turned it down. He would not do it because he was not guilty of this crime, and if he pled guilty, he and those he loves would forever carry that stigma with them. And the guilty person would be free to commit the same crime again. Michael knew that it would affect more than just himself. He was willing to risk prison because he believed that you, as jurors, would do the right thing.

"It is up to you to determine whether or not the state has presented sufficient evidence to find Michael guilty beyond a reasonable doubt. Clearly they haven't. They've provided sufficient passion, I give them that. But nothing to prove him guilty. I believe that, in this case, you must do more than find Michael not guilty. You need to find him innocent. Michael has already lost his scholarship, a job he cares about, and his good name because of these false accusations. It is not within your power to restore all of that. But you might be able to restore some of it."

Amanda walked over to the desk and took a drink of water, then returned to the jury. "What I find most ironic about this whole trial is that Michael is probably more sickened by what happened to Henri than anyone in this room. More so than those who accuse him. More than that ignorant lynch mob ranting outside for Michael to be punished. Michael knew Henri and cared about him. And cared for him.

"The prosecution has urged you to send a resounding message to society that we will not tolerate the kind of abuse illustrated by this case. I agree. We must not tolerate the abuse of an individual's right to justice. If that is too abstract a concept for you, then try this one on—close your eyes and pretend, just for a moment, that it is not Michael sitting there, but your own son. Your own grandson." Just then Amanda's voice faltered, and I knew it was not part of the show. It was how she felt. She looked over at me and her eyes were moist, then she took a breath and turned back to the jury. "Michael didn't plead guilty, because he believed that you would do the right thing. For God's sake, do the right thing."

Amanda walked back to her seat and sat down. There was a palpable dissonance ringing throughout the room.

The judge turned to the prosecution. "Rebuttal?"

The prosecution waived with a simple head shake, and then, at the judge's directive, the jury rose and filed out of the room. They returned an hour and forty-five minutes later.

chapter thirty

The Verdict

"How often the course of a life is changed in one pulse of a heart."

Excerpt from Esther Huish's Diary

"You may be seated," the bailiff said. The judge looked out over the courtroom.

"It is my understanding that the jury has completed its deliberation," the judge said. He faced the counsel. "Is everyone in the courtroom who needs to be?"

"Yes, Your Honor," Amanda and the prosecutor said almost in unison.

"Call the jury in."

The courtroom fell silent as the jurors filed back into their seats, inversely to the pulsing of my heart. As much as I had anticipated this moment, I was now ready to postpone it for another day, preferably indefinitely. Faye leaned forward and put her arm around me, and under the table Amanda reached over and took my hand.

The judge waited until the jurors had settled into place. "Do you have a foreperson?"

A man said, "Yes, Your Honor." He was a large, well-fed man with a striped, short-sleeve permanent press shirt, sweat stained beneath the armpits. He spoke with a rancher's drawl and it was easier to envision him with a John Deere hat than a foreman's title.

"Would that be you, Mr. Olsen?"

"Yes, Your Honor."

"Is it correct that the jury has reached a unanimous verdict?"

"Yes, sir."

"Please hand that verdict to my clerk." The man rose and delivered the envelope to the clerk, who returned one of the forms back to him and handed the other to the judge. He glanced up from the paper. "Mr. Olsen, is this in fact the verdict of the jury?"

"Yes, Your Honor."

The judge looked at the jurors dispassionately, then said, "Please read the verdict."

The man breathed in deeply. "We, the jurors in the above case, find the defendant not guilty of criminal homicide."

There was a cry in the audience. I threw my arms around Amanda, and a broad smile spread across her face. "You were right," she said, grinning, and the emotion she had invested in my behalf was evident. Faye embraced me from behind and I turned around, and she wet my face with her tears. The foreman remained standing, looking tentatively at the judge.

"Is there something else you would like to say before I dismiss the jury?" the judge asked.

"Your Honor, we don't know if you allow this sort of thing, but we've written a statement."

The judge pounded his gavel against the courtroom's clamor. "Attention, please." The room quieted. "Please hand your statement to the clerk."

The clerk took the notice from the foreman and relayed it to the judge. The judge reviewed the statement, then returned it to the clerk.

"The clerk will read the statement," he announced. The clerk cleared his throat.

"This jury has found Michael Keddington falsely accused of a horrendous crime, which he has courageously defied. We are proud of his stand for truth and commend him for his faith in justice. We are proud that he is a member of our community and hope that the press, the Arcadia Care Facility, and any other organization that have wrongfully denied him of his rights and privileges or censured him in any way will take great strides to make whole the damage that has been caused him through these false charges."

I watched the foreman during the reading, and when the clerk finished, the foreman looked over at me and I mouthed a thank-you, and his eyes were strong and kind and he tipped his head to me. The judge commended the jury for their labors and dismissed them.

"I lied, you know," Amanda said to me as the courtroom cleared.

I looked at her quizzically. "About what?"

"When I told you that I graduated with the top twenty of my class."

"You didn't?"

"In a sense. Top twenty percentile."

I hugged her again. "I owe you."

"You can come tend after I have the baby." She grinned. "We both owe that to Phil."

I laughed, and Faye did not speak, but stood holding my hand, tears still evident on her cheeks. I put my arms around her and held her.

Helen walked up to me; her face showed a curious mix of gratitude and sadness. "Congratulations, Michael. I'm sorry that you had to learn about Esther this way."

"Were you with her when she went?"

"No. Sharon was. She said she went peacefully." She touched my shoulder. "When things have settled for you, I'd like to talk to you about your job. We're all ready for you to come back."

"I'll give you a call. Thank you for your testimony."

"Don't mention it."

I turned to Amanda. "Are we done here?"

"You're free to go," she said. "Except I'm driving."

Faye said to Amanda, "Thank you for saving my man."

Amanda smiled. "He was worth saving."

The three of us walked out together, passing through a gauntlet of reporters, who volleyed questions at Amanda and me until a distraught Starley Richards appeared outside the courtroom next to his daughter, presenting a bigger catch. As the paparazzi diminished, Faye said, "I hope my parents aren't watching the news tonight."

"Or any of their friends?" Amanda asked.

Faye sighed. "I guess I'll have some explaining to do when I come back for spring break."

"When are you leaving?" I asked.

She leaned against me. "There's a flight out tonight."

"How do you know that?"

"I always weigh my options," she said matter-of-factly.

"You already have your tickets?"

She looked into my eyes and smiled. "No. I wasn't that confident." She took my hand. "I'll be back next Saturday for spring break."

I glanced at my watch. "What time is the flight?"

"We have until nine-thirty."

"I'll get you two back to the house," Amanda said. "Phil and I have a date tonight as well."

chapter thirty-one

Esther's Room

"I have wondered if I am trying to force a life. While the life I lead may not match the picture in my head, perhaps the one offered me is just as full of joy, its pigments just as bright, just not what I expected."

Excerpt from Esther Huish's Diary

Faye's departure was a vast improvement over our previous one, though I've never found much good in good-byes. At least, this time, she was the last to board the plane. The drive home gave me time to reflect, and my mind reeled in as many directions as the slush that spun from my tires. It was hard to believe that the trial was over—that the hatchet that had wavered precariously had truly been withdrawn. That realization gave way to a peculiar new emotional cycle: I would think to share my joy with Esther, and then the reality of her loss would bring me back down.

When I reached Ogden, I took the first city exit and drove up to the canyon. It had been too long since I had stepped foot in the Arcadia.

The hour was late, past eleven-thirty, and the Arcadia was darkened and silent, though I could hear the drone of an unattended television in the dayroom. Inside the foyer Sharon stood next to a female orderly who was unfamiliar to me, and the two women stopped talking as I entered. Sharon immediately walked over and embraced me.

"You don't know how worried we've all been."

"Thank you, Sharon."

She then stepped back and her countenance fell in sudden realization of why I had come. "You came for Esther. You still don't know . . ."

"I know she's gone. Helen told me."

"I'm sorry, Michael."

"Helen said that you were with her at her passing."

"I was by her side for the last few hours."

"Was she coherent?"

She shook her head. "No. She lost coherency shortly after midnight. I had to give her morphine. But she went peacefully."

I frowned at the thought of her passing, and Sharon squeezed my hand. "I'm sorry you couldn't be with her. I know she would have wanted that."

"I'd like to go up to her room."

"Of course. It's been locked. I'll give you my key." Sharon handed me a key from her own ring. I turned to go, but as I mounted the first step she asked me in sudden remembrance, "Do you know who Thomas is?"

I turned back. "Thomas? Why?"

"Before she went she called out to him. I just thought he might like to know."

"No," I said sadly. "It won't make any difference."

I turned and climbed the stairway. The third floor appeared abandoned, as it usually did at night, though I could see a dim light emanating from the nurses' station and hear the hushed murmur of someone speaking on the telephone. I stopped outside Esther's room in the shadowed doorway, and there was a coldness there, perhaps a product of my own expectation, but it felt real and it gave me pause. I inserted the brass key, turned it, then suddenly wavered. It felt wrong that I might open the door and Esther not be there. I suddenly questioned if I should enter the room—if, perhaps, trespassing it would violate the memories that we had shared, rewriting over them with a hollow, lonely script. Ultimately, the same memories that I feared were threatened were what drew me back inside, to illuminate those memories again with the props that had surrounded our experiences and the time we shared together. I slowly pushed open the door.

The small, vaulted room was darkened and its only illumination came from the moon's reflection off the sloped, snow-draped canyon walls, through the unveiled glass panes. I closed the door behind me and looked around, alone in the silence. There was no sound or motion, just the mellifluous flow of memory and Esther's final words still alive in my mind. Her final words. They could not have been better selected, and I then realized that she knew it would be our last moment shared. Perhaps not consciously, but instinctively, as the migrating bird knows when its journey is done. I picked up the portrait of Esther as a young woman and wondered if this was what she looked like now—if she had shed the decrepit shell of age and resumed a glorious spirit alive in the prime of her life.

Through the course of my life I have come to believe that life is not lived chronologically, by the sweep of a clock's hand or the sway of its pendulum, but rather, experientially, as a ladder or stair, each experience stacked upon the previous, delivering us to loftier planes. Perhaps this best describes my concept of God—the architect of that divine ascent, the hidden arm that slashes our swath through the overgrown flora of destiny, best revealed in the evidence of our lives.

Esther was a part of that divine tutelage, and it was as if she had come to my life for this one moment—this one vital step of my own spiritual evolution. I could not help but wonder if she was more angel than woman. A sad angel.

There was more to see in the room, each artifact a key to opening some memory. Hanging on the wall above her bed were dried flowers, the winter roses I had sent the day after we visited Thomas. Then I grinned. Just as dry was the still-uneaten fruitcake, now approaching a state of petrification.

There was a soft knock, then the door slowly opened and Helen walked into the room.

"Sharon said I would find you here." She looked at me solemnly. "You okay?"

"I'll be all right. How about you? Will your testimony threaten your position here?"

"Starley Richards has more to worry about these days than me." She stepped closer. "I'm sorry I had to act so cold. I suspected Alice from the beginning, but I knew it would take some doing to bring her down and that I better at least appear impartial."

I suddenly understood. "You told Amanda about Alice's drugs . . ."

"Unlike Alice, I never forget a resident. I was with the police when they searched your locker. When I saw Lucille Haymond's name on the medicine bottle, I knew we had her."

"I don't know how to thank you."

"I do. By coming back to work for me. You are missed here."

"I'll think about it. I have a lot to think about these days." I looked around the room at Esther's possessions. "What will you do with all this?"

"Usually when there's not a next of kin, it's sold for charity. But Esther had other plans for her things." She took an envelope from her pocket. "Esther had me help her with two letters. The one for court and this one just in case."

I took the letter from her.

"You know what it says?"

Helen nodded. "Esther dictated it to me. But I'll leave you alone with her." She walked over and hugged me. "You're a good man, Michael Keddington. God knows we could use more men like you." She turned and walked to the door and stopped. "Esther's funeral is tomorrow at ten at the Baptist church down by the cemetery. If you're willing, I think it would be appropriate for you to say something." I nodded and she closed the door behind her. I turned on the small shaded bed lamp, then turned off the main light and went and sat down on the bed next to Esther's chair, where I had read the obituaries each day. Before I opened the letter I ran my hand across the near arm of the chair as if a portion of her spirit lingered still.

My dearest Michael,

I would so rather say these things to your face, but as we both know, life doesn't often take requests. So I've asked Helen to help me with this letter. Just in case. I suppose this is a will of sorts. First, I do not know yet the outcome of the trial. I cannot know if you are reading this in a cage. I can only hope my letter and the signatures of your friends were of some benefit. I have faith that you will be free, so I shall write this letter as such and not take counsel from my fears.

I would like you to have my letters and my diaries. They are the scars of my heart's wound. A heart you helped to heal. They hold my deepest feelings and that is what, most of all, I would like to leave with you. I also bequeath to you my furniture and my Bible. The furniture is hand carved and antique. The bureau was crafted by Marius Morrell, who gained some notoriety as a joiner, so there may be some value to it. It is sturdy at any rate. The Bible belonged to my father. It is old but its value is in its words, not material.

In the bottom drawer of my bureau, buried beneath my letters, is a leather portfolio. For years, William and I put every extra penny we earned into war bonds which were meant to be used for Matthew's care after we were both gone. I have not had much need for money and the bonds have long since matured. There should be enough to pay for your schooling and some of your expenses.

In the top drawer of the bureau is a velvet pouch containing two heirlooms. The first is my locket. I would like you to return it to Betheltown for me—to lay it by the hearth of the fireplace where I left my love so many years ago. I had once thought to be buried in Betheltown, but I no longer hold that desire. The locket will be sufficient. I have helped Helen to draw a map. I am certain that the roads will be grown over, but you will know the place.

In the pouch is also the engagement ring of Thomas's that I retrieved from the fireplace's hearth. What you do with it is for you to decide. I have not been one to share advice (coming from me, what could it be worth?) but this much I know. You are good. And there is more to that than is contained in all the world's treasure-houses. To come from the fringes of humanity and remain clean of cynicism is as high an ambition as *a soul may aspire to. Do not be afraid to choose good for yourself, Michael. I know you have never considered this, it is not your way, but Faye would be truly fortunate to have you.*

I am proud of you, Michael. As proud, I suspect, as your own mother might be. If I am to see her in some other realm I shall offer her my gratitude for lending me her son for a while. I do not know what more I could say than what I wrote in my letter to the jury—if my son were whole, I would have hoped that he would someday be like you.

God does allow us second chances. But sometimes they're just best given to someone else.

Go well, my dear friend,
Esther

chapter thirty-two

The Locket

"If the errors of my life have profited me one great truth it is this: believe. Believe in your destiny and the star from which it shines. Believe you have been sent from God as an arrow pulled from his own bow.

It is the single universal trait which the great of this earth have all shared, while the shadows are fraught with ghosts who roam the winds with mournful wails of regret on their lips.

Believe as if your life depended upon it, for indeed it does."

Excerpt from Esther Huish's Diary

Bethel, Utah. April 2, 1989

There is a spectral air to an abandoned town—the inexplicable feeling that one is being watched, not by such reptilian life as thrives in desolation, but rather the wraiths of the land's past inhabitants, immured in the lusts that brought them to the territory and hold sway still. I have felt similar movings on the ground of a memorial battlefield where each step of earth was once claimed, bled for, and is now bequeathed to those that bought the land with their mortality. I can't prove it but I know what I felt.

There was no way of knowing how long it had been since the forgotten town had been trespassed, but there was not so much as a clay print of a tire track or the toss of beer cans or cigarette butts that unfailingly denotes mankind's presence in nature. If the town had seen life in the past decade, it was likely not of the human variety.

Faye and I climbed out of the car near what was the town's largest surviving structure, a sandstone church of spectacular proportions. Its weathered, adobe brick walls rose more than twenty feet, still holding aloft its canopied bell tower, though its bell was absent and likely melted down for its metal. In a town of ore and smelters, all metal objects were considered malleable to the moment's need.

We trespassed the dim, palatial hall, surprised to find the remnants of the church's original furnishings. Its pews were tipped backward and it was not hard to imagine their fall and clatter like a row of dominoes. Singular rays of sunlight shone from cracks in the walls, spotlighting portions of the dusty interior. Above, from its shadowed lair, a moonfaced barn owl stoically followed our intrusion.

We returned to daylight and walked to the rear of the church, to a fallen corral and the collapsed remains of two buildings we could not identify, though I suspected the structure nearest the corral had once been the blacksmith's shop. I have read that the Shoshone Indians did not bury their dead, but rather collapsed their homes around them, and this too had that appearance.

Some thirty yards back, the timbered mouth of an abandoned mine gaped from the side of the terraced mountain, partially obscured behind a line of cedars.

Neither Faye nor I said much as we perused the ruins, as if held silent by some mutual thought of reverence for the deceased township. Faye took my hand as we crossed the square to the village's last vestige of seeming integrity, a two-story saltbox edifice that I guessed to be the Bethel Boarding House and Inn. The inn had an elevated wooden porch with spindle columns rising to a shingled overhang. The steep, gabled roof, miraculously still intact, was bookended by simple sandstone-and-mortar chimneys. The clay walls, like its roof, were remarkably well preserved. A single swath of wooden stairs climbed the banistered porch.

"I think this is the inn," I said. I placed a tentative step on the stairs' first plank, which gave slightly. "The wood's soft. Just watch your step."

"I always watch my step," Faye said without looking up. She entered the narrow doorway behind me.

The room was wide and low ceilinged, above a scarred wood-plank floor. A stairway climbed to the rooms of the second floor, rising above an arched doorway that led to the kitchen and the innkeeper's quarters. Against the far wall the broad, brookstone–set hearth of the fireplace remained, its pinewood mantel fallen faceward to the floor. In its firebox remained a charred log and its fall of ashes.

"This is the place," I said, turning to Faye. "This is where Esther lost her chance for love."

Faye came and stood by my side. I squatted down and lifted the mantelpiece, leaning it back against the stone hearth, then stepped backward, imagining how it was once seen by those gathered to its light for drink and company—the newly arrived prospectors whose tongues wagged of still-unearthed riches and the more weary voices of the seasoned miners, who spoke of lost homes and loves, cured of their optimism but not the gold's addiction. And I could imagine two lovers, a frightened young woman with fallow hair and an olive-complexioned young man, vulnerable, on his knees, pleading before the hearth the evening before his departure for war. And the ring he flung into its yellow flames as he left her side.

I took from my back pocket the aged, velvet pouch, untied its leather drawstring, and drew from it Esther's beautiful locket, allowing its chain, an ethereal braid of rose gold, to dangle from my palm. I unclasped the tiny case, exposing the two miniature portraits.

Faye leaned her head into my shoulder, then slid her hand into mine, gazing with me at the yellowed photographs within the exquisite heirloom.

"Esther was a beautiful young woman," Faye said softly.

"She was always beautiful," I replied, still staring at the piece. I crouched down and, with the back of my hand, brushed back the ashes from the stone floor of the firebox, then laid the open locket on the hearth, carefully spreading its chain in an awkward circle.

Faye stared at the jewelry, wondering at the meaning of what we had come so far to accomplish. I rose, turning slowly from the hearth, and Faye moved close, wrapping both arms around my waist. After a moment she said gently, "We came for her."

She gazed on me in quiet repose, her dark, almond eyes deeply piercing, searching. I drew her close and pulled her head into my chest. I kissed the top of her head. "No. We came for us."

I released her, then again brought out the velvet bag and spilled its remaining content into the palm of my hand. Esther's ring. It shone exquisitely, the emerald marquis playfully reflecting the room's light. I took Faye's hand and, silenced by my own uncertainty of her reaction, slipped the band onto her finger. For a full minute she stared down at the ring, and though I could not see her eyes, I saw that her hand slightly trembled.

A gentle breeze danced over the faded drapery that hung in strips from the paneless windows, and Faye slowly looked up into my face and her eyes were moist, and I knew she understood the great healing that had taken place. A slight smile rose upon her lips.

"What took you so long?"

I lifted her chin and softly kissed her. I began to replace the pouch when I perceived that there was something still inside. A folded piece of paper. I took it out, anticipating, perhaps, a note from Esther. I unfolded the sheet and examined it more closely. It was the torn-out page of a book—the book Esther had once recited from to me—*Paradise Lost.* I smiled in understanding and for Esther's wisdom, then read the passage out loud to Faye.

> *Some natural tears they dropped, but wiped them soon;*
> *The world was all before them, where to choose*
> *Their place of rest, and providence their guide;*
> *They, hand in hand, with wandering steps and slow,*
> *Through Eden took their solitary way.*

I took Faye's hand, and we reemerged into the dismal terrain to return to our car. A breeze again breathed through the town, and I held Faye's door, then went to my own, pausing once more for the journey and the memory of the woman who had brought me through it. Then we forever left Bethel to its ghosts.

About the Author

Richard Paul Evans is the bestselling author of *The Christmas Box, Timepiece,* and *The Letter* as well as the children's book, *The Christmas Candle.* He is also the founder of The Christmas Box House International, an organization dedicated to building shelters for abused children. He lives in Salt Lake City, Utah, with his wife, Keri, and their five children. He is currently working on his next novel.

Please send Richard Paul Evans's correspondence to:

P.O. Box 1416
Salt Lake City, UT 84110

Or visit his Web site at http://www.thechristmasbox.com